# anne cassidy
# innocent

# anne cassidy
# innocent

*Hodder*
*Children's*
*Books*

a division of Hodder Headline Limited

A Catalogue record for this book is available from the British Library

ISBN 0 340 88200 X

Typeset in Baskerville by Avon DataSet Ltd,
Bidford-on-Avon, Warwickshire

Printed and bound in Great Britain by
Bookmarque Ltd, Croydon, Surrey

The paper and board used in this paperback by Hodder Children's
Books are natural recyclable products made from wood grown
in sustainable forests. The manufacturing processes conform to the
environmental regulations of the country of origin.

Hodder Children's Books
a division of Hodder Headline Ltd
338 Euston Road
London NW1 3BH

# Sunday

# 1

The crash was hard to explain. An early evening in July, the traffic on the motorway was light. A car transporter had moved into the middle lane and was trying to pass a caravan that was trudging along at fifty miles an hour. The lorry driver, Paul Sullivan, had dark glasses on and wasn't bothered by the sun, which hung heavy in the sky like a ripe orange. He was listening to a compilation tape, the volume high. For a few moments he imagined himself in a sports car, open top, gliding along a beach road. Then he came back to reality and laughed at himself. It was exactly two weeks and three days until he and his family were due to go to Portugal.

He glanced in his wing mirror and noticed a car coming up in the fast lane. One minute it seemed miles back and then it was nudging his shoulder. A Jaguar, postbox red, it seemed to nose past him without touching the ground. Like a low-flying aircraft it sped away and disappeared under a footbridge on the horizon. Having passed the caravan Paul put his indicator on to move into the inside lane. Just then the music changed. A throbbing drum and insistent guitar made him move around in his seat with sheer pleasure. It was ages since he'd heard this one. He sung along with the words. Up ahead he noticed people on the footbridge. He felt his vehicle slowing and realized that he was going up a slope. He put his foot down, easing the heavy load into the inside lane, feeling the weight of the cars on his back. The caravan was close behind him and the song was reaching its climax and he hummed along with the final chorus.

It wasn't a crowd on the footbridge he noticed that much. Three, four maybe? What a life! A glorious Sunday summer evening and all these young lads had to do was hang around a motorway. At that age he was out pulling girls. Sex and cars and music. Those were his pastimes. And he hadn't worn too badly. He still had his hair. Not many of his mates could say that.

The stone hit the windscreen, making a loud crack. Like the sound of a whip. It startled him and in the blink of an eye the glass in front of him splintered, blurring his vision and filling his stomach with a sick feeling. He couldn't see, didn't see the motorbike that buzzed past and swung in front of him. The lorry swerved and his chest and shoulders froze for a second, paralysed with fright. With trembling arms he began to feed the steering wheel through his hands, aware of some invisible wave pulling his great weight to one side, threatening to capsize him in the middle of the road.

That's when he saw, out the corner of his eye, the blue minibus sailing past him.

His foot slammed on and off the brake pedal; three, four

times. His arms, stiff like rods, were holding on to the steering wheel, as if to push it away. The brakes screamed, the sound piercing him from ear to ear. He felt a heavy weight pulling him to one side and his stomach rose up into his throat as the road turned sideways in front of him. He closed his eyes. He couldn't help it. All he could hear were the sounds of braking cars squealing behind him, like a flock of angry gulls.

Then it was silent.

# Monday

## 2

I didn't find the usual mess in the kitchen when I got up. That surprised me. I'd heard Brad come in after midnight. He was noisy, moving around, opening and shutting drawers. I'd assumed he'd been making a late night snack. But there was no sign that he'd made anything for himself.

He tripped on the stairs, I heard that much. He swore and I heard a slur in his voice. He was drunk. He'd been like it before. Emily would roll her eyes if I told her. She disapproved of most things my brother did.

I made some toast. Two slices cut into triangles, one covered with honey, the other with apricot jam. I put them on a china plate and carried it through to the living-room. I sat in my usual armchair in front of the television. I picked a piece up by its corner and bit a neat half moon out of it, brushing my knees for any crumbs. After a few moments of careful chewing I noticed something shiny on the carpet, just under the sofa. I got down on my knees and reached for it. A silver hoop. My mislaid earring. I should have been pleased to see it but instead it gave me a twinge of nerves and Denny Scott's face came into my head. I picked it up, held it to my lips for a moment and then put it in my jeans pocket.

I sighed and reached for the remote and pressed the news channel button. The sound was off and I watched the newsreader mouthing for a while and then there was film of a motorway, the screen showing cars lying on the road, and a motorbike, on its side by a giant lorry. A crash. I watched in silence as a footbridge came into shot and a presenter stood talking into a mike.

Normally this was my favourite time of day. My dad, a computer technician, worked early shifts and always left around six-thirty leaving me and Brad asleep. At seven I usually got up, showered and dressed and spent some time on my own. Even when I didn't have to *be* anywhere I liked to get up early. The house was quiet and felt empty. I loved the tranquillity. I could make my breakfast without Brad getting in the way, leaving the fridge door open, the carton of milk out on the side, his tea bag on the work surface, wet and soggy. And none of his moaning about his work or his car or his lack of money.

At half past seven, most mornings, I sat and luxuriated in front of the television, flicking from one channel to the other, picking up snippets of news and getting myself ready for another day.

This morning I should have been in an even better mood because it was the official start of the school summer holidays. My best friend Emily and I had lots of plans. We were going to decorate her bedroom. We had galleries and museums to visit; research to do to prepare for our 'A' level courses. These things had been planned for ages and Emily had made a kind of timetable for us both. She'd printed it off and I had a copy on my bedroom notice-board. Denny had remarked on it. *That Emily thinks she's your boss*, he'd said.

But something had happened in the last couple of weeks that had taken the shine off our arrangements. The thought of trudging round museums didn't hold the same wonder for me. The 'A' levels that were starting in September no longer seemed such a milestone.

Part of me wanted to call it *Love*.

The more sensible side of me didn't know what to call it.

I shifted around in the chair trying to get comfortable. My uneaten toast was cold and soft. I tried to make myself concentrate at the silent television screen which was now showing what looked like another car accident. A policeman was standing in front of a bus stop, waving cars by. The camera showed a close-up of a street sign. Bunches of flowers were tied to a nearby lamppost.

*Love*. It wasn't the right word and it didn't really describe the things that were happening. I thought back to the previous day. Denny, my brother's best mate, calling round deliberately when he knew that my brother was out.

'Your dad around?' he'd said, sitting on the settee beside me.

It wasn't a real question because he knew full well that my dad was out. He didn't even wait for me to give any kind of answer, just pulled me towards him and began kissing me hard on the mouth, his hands holding the tops of my arms so tightly I'd thought there'd be bruises.

'Use your tongue,' he'd whispered, pulling back for a split second. 'The way I taught you.'

And I did. And somehow we slithered on to the floor and he'd ended up on top of me, pinning me down, his leg moving between mine. He had other things to teach me, I knew that. I lay my head back on the floor and closed my eyes. I was ready for it. Ready for anything. But the ring of the telephone startled us both. It sounded like a bell at the end of a boxing round. We both stopped, him darting back to the settee, me scrambling for the phone in the hallway, vaguely aware that one of my earrings was gone.

I wanted it to be love. But how could Denny Scott have feelings for me?

He was nineteen, I was sixteen. He worked, I went to school. He was good-looking, funny, strong, brainy. I was too tall and skinny with no breasts to speak of. I was shy and blushed like a beetroot whenever I felt awkward or stressed. I was happiest talking to Emily about books or writing stories of my own. He talked easily to anyone, making jokes, joining in with discussions.

On top of all this Denny already had a girlfriend.

I'd seen him with her on Saturday evening. Brad was giving me a lift to Emily's house. We drove through Epping Forest and stopped off at High Beech, a local beauty spot. Brad wanted to give Denny some money he owed him. We found his car in the pub car park. He and Tania were leaning against it. He was talking into her ear, his fingers playing with the neck of her T-shirt. Her body just fitted neatly by his and she had a hint of a smile on her face, as though his words were giving her pleasure.

It made my legs go weak to see them. I had my copy of *Jane Eyre* on my lap and I made a half-hearted attempt to read it. It was in preparation for my 'A' level and I had already highlighted some sections of the first chapter. There was a stone weight in my stomach though and my eyes were pulled back to the couple by the car. As he kissed her I moved around in my seat, flicking through the pages of my book, my thighs feeling as though they were on fire.

And then, twenty-four hours later, he was next to me on my living-room floor, his breath burning my neck, my earring rubbing against the carpet. Just the memory of it made my throat ache.

On the screen, a reporter was talking to a policeman. I watched the woman's red lips moving and the policeman's head nodding, one of his hands smoothing back his hair. Across the bottom of the screen was a ribbon of colour and words moving from right to left. I made myself concentrate on them. Anything to get my mind off Denny. *Are drugs responsible for the rise in road traffic accidents?* I sighed. Death and misery on the news. I reached for the remote and clicked the 'off' button. The screen went blank.

I picked up my uneaten food and was about to take it through to the kitchen when there was a knock at the front door. A second later the bell rang. Then the knocking and the bell began to sound at the same time, as if someone was in a panic. I made my way out and pulled the door open. Two police officers stood there. One of them was in uniform, with steel-grey hair and a large stomach. The other one I knew: Tony Haskins. He'd been involved with Brad before.

'What? What's happened? Is my dad all right?' I said, thinking that there had been an accident.

'It's not about your dad, Charlotte,' Tony Haskins said, a look of concern on his face, 'This is Constable Pearson. We're here to talk to Bradley.'

'Why?' I said, my relief quickly replaced with anxiety about my brother.

'We need to talk to him. It's important. Is he in?'

'What's he done?' I said, pulling the door over a bit, trying to exclude them, my heart sinking into my shoes.

'Is Bradley at home or not?' the other officer said, clearing his throat, his voice booming out. 'We need to speak with him on a matter of some urgency.'

I was about to answer when I heard footsteps from behind me. I turned and saw my brother halfway down the stairs wearing only his boxer shorts and holding a T-shirt scrunched up in one hand. His hair was sticking out and he looked half asleep. When he saw the police he stopped.

'Brad,' I said, pointing at the door.

Brad looked pale, his skin like wax. His face dropped and he pulled the T-shirt over his head and covered himself up.

'Bradley Simon?' the older policeman said.

Brad's eyes flicked from one policeman to the other. Then he looked back up the stairs and down along the hallway as though he were considering what to do. For a moment I thought he might turn and run away, up the stairs or along the hallway and out the back door.

'Brad?' I said.

His shoulders slumped and he stood sullenly, as though he was a schoolboy about to be told off.

'Bradley, we need to talk to you. Down at the station. Now.'

'What do they want, Brad?' I said.

'Nothing,' Brad said, shaking his head. 'I'm not saying nothing. I'll be back before you know it. All right if I get my shoes?'

'As long as I can come with you, son,' the older policeman said.

Brad turned back up the stairs. The policeman followed him slowly, each step making a sound under his weight. When he was at the top I turned and glared at Tony Haskins. He'd shaved his head so that his bald patch was less noticeable. He was wearing a suit which made him look formal. He saw me looking.

'I'm in court later. I've had to smarten up.'

'What's going on?' I said, ignoring his attempt at conversation. 'What's he supposed to have done?'

'I can't say, Charlotte. You know I can't say.'

'I'll know soon enough!' I said, exasperated.

'We're investigating a motorway incident.'

'Motorway?' I said, puzzled, something clicking in the back of my head.

Brad was coming down the stairs behind the older policeman. There was a murmur of voices, mostly the policeman's.

'A big crash, yesterday evening. Casualties,' Tony said, his voice dropping.

'What's that got to do with Brad?' I demanded.

'Some kids were throwing stones at passing cars. One of them hit the lorry.'

'You don't think Brad was . . .'

'Leave it, Charlie. Don't say nothing,' my brother said.

'What about Dad?' I said.

In my head I saw my dad's face hardening at the news, his mouth closing tightly as he tried to control his annoyance with Brad.

'Don't ring him. I'll probably be home in a couple of hours.'

Brad put an unlit cigarette in his mouth.

'No smoking in the car, son,' the uniformed officer said.

'Ring me,' I shouted, as he got into the back seat, tossing the cigarette on to the ground.

I watched the car until it turned out of the road, a feeling of gloom settling on me. Brad, in trouble with the police. It wasn't the first time. I thought of the television news I'd been forced to watch minutes earlier. A lorry on its side on the tarmac, a nearby motorcycle and cars strewn around. Kids throwing stones. I shook my head. Brad wasn't a kid. Throwing stones off a motorway footbridge wasn't his style. Drinking too much, nicking stuff, chasing after girls, getting into fights. These were Brad's pastimes.

Throwing stones at moving cars.

I shook my head, a feeling of certainty taking over me. It just wasn't *Brad*.

# 3

A couple of hours later I was on a bus heading for the town centre and the police station. The bus was packed and I was standing, wedged up against a window, looking out as the streets went slowly past. The bus kept stopping and starting, making it hard to stand upright, and I was jostled by people squeezing past to get off and others edging past to get on. The sky was grey with wall-to-wall clouds. It suited my mood.

I wondered how Brad was feeling.

He was probably sitting in a room waiting to be interviewed, smoking or drinking tea from a polystyrene cup. None of it would be new to him. He'd been in that same station before, a number of times: caught in possession of cannabis three times; receiving stolen property twice (mobile phones); one charge of public affray and one of assault both stemming from his attraction to fighting. There were several other brushes with the law that hadn't resulted in anything. It was true to say that my brother was *known to the police*.

This time though, I felt less concerned and more angry. Brad wasn't the type to stand on a footbridge and throw stones down at oncoming drivers. He was a driver himself.

He would never do anything so dangerous. The police were looking for someone young, tall, skinny with short dark hair. Brad fitted the picture.

Emily wouldn't be surprised. I'd considered calling her and telling her what had happened but had decided against it. Emily didn't need any excuse to disapprove of my brother. She didn't have much time for Denny either, lumping the two of them together as *typical laddish types*.

They were different though. They'd been friends since school but they seemed ill-matched. Brad worked as a car mechanic and was perpetually scruffy. Denny worked in an office and wore smart clothes all the time. Brad liked to go to the pub. He drank a lot and often couldn't get up in the morning saying he felt sick. Denny was rarely drunk. I knew that he sometimes smoked dope, using his thumb and forefingers to make skinny roll-ups while Brad swigged back can after can of beer. My brother had a short fuse. He took offence at the smallest thing: a missed space in a car park, the man in the newsagent's serving him slowly, someone looking at him oddly in the ticket queue at the tube station. He thought nothing of picking an argument with complete strangers. Denny was the peacemaker, always finding a reason to calm things down.

Dennis Scott. I closed my eyes as a feeling of longing washed over me. Denny and Charlie. Why not? He was only three years older than me. He was a friend. I'd known him for years. I knew that he loved cars, always working on his, cleaning it and buying new parts for it. I knew that he hated his job and only stayed because the money was good.

He was a good, loyal friend to my brother. And he'd liked me for years. He called me *Little Miss Innocent* even though I wasn't little any more.

But Denny already had a girlfriend.

I opened my eyes. Outside it was raining, the drops just starting to mark the glass. Now was not the time to think of me and Denny. Brad had been arrested. He was in trouble. I had to *focus*. I stared into the rain, pushing Denny from my thoughts.

The bus was inching forward bit by bit, its engine wheezing. I slumped against the window. There was no rush. I knew how it worked. I'd been in this situation before. The first time I'd been frantic, imagining my brother in a cell, being mistreated, fitted up, his young life wasted in some grimy prison. But with each new brush with the law my feelings dimmed. I was upset but deep down I wasn't surprised.

I looked over to the other side of the road where the cars were moving freely, their windscreen wipers slapping back and forth. Through the traffic I saw flowers attached to the railings at the edge of the pavement. They were brightly coloured, the blooms standing proudly out, trumpeting the grey street, perked up by the fine drizzle. A child's teddy bear sat on the pavement among them. I frowned. It was a tiny altar to some other road accident. It made me think of the motorway crash, one car smashing into another. I'd put News 24 on again while I was getting ready but the report had not been repeated. It was a big lorry, I remembered, and some cars and a motorbike.

A beeping sound made me reach into my bag for my mobile. On the screen was the word *Dad*. I hesitated. If I answered it I would have to tell him about Brad. There was sure to be a row. I sighed and shoved it back in my bag and started to move towards the exit for my stop.

The police station stood on its own away from nearby shops. I pressed the entry button and waited until a buzzer sounded so that I could enter. The reception was like a wide corridor with a counter at one end and a line of plastic chairs down the side. A uniformed policeman was on the desk. In the chairs there were a couple of black girls and an older white man. The girls were whispering and leaning away from the man as though he was nothing to do with them.

I walked forward. I'd been in this waiting area before.

'Yes?' the policeman on reception said.

His lips were bunched up with expectation and his eyes dropped down to some papers on the counter in front of him.

'Mr Haskins asked me to come in? I'm Charlotte Simon?'

I said it sweetly, using my full name. As if I had an appointment. I knew that if I asked for my brother I'd be told to take a seat and would probably sit waiting for hours.

'Regarding?' he said, continuing to look down.

'A road traffic matter,' I said, smiling, trying to convey confidence even though I didn't feel it.

He gave a great sigh as if it was all too much trouble, then, without making any eye contact at all, he picked up the telephone. *Have a nice day*, I wanted to say but kept quiet. Tony Haskins appeared a few moments later. He came briskly out from behind the counter, smoothing his tie down with the flat of his hand, and seemed out of breath. He punched in a security code and led me into a small boxroom with a table and two chairs. I sat down and looked expectantly at him. He stayed standing and didn't say a word. Behind him was a giant poster. It showed a hooded man walking through undergrowth at the back of some houses. The words **We've Got Our Eye on You** were underneath the logo for Neighbourhood Watch.

'I'm due in court in an hour so I've got to be quick,' he said, pushing his sleeve up to look at his watch.

'I want to know when Brad's coming home.'

'I don't know, Charlotte. It's out of my hands now.'

'But you could find out. You could ask.'

He shook his head, brushing fluff off his jacket.

'I can't interfere. It's a big case. A serious accident. People have been hurt.'

'Brad's got nothing to do with it. He wouldn't . . .'

'There were witnesses . . .'

'Who?' I said hopelessly.

'He's being interviewed. That's all I can tell you,' he said, shuffling about, looking down at his shoes.

'I'll wait for him.'

'It'll be hours. Why don't you go home and ring later. There may even be developments,' he said.

*Developments.* That was police-speak for an arrest and a charge. I felt this ball of indignation in my chest. I got up and walked out of the room, letting the door swing behind me.

'Brad is innocent,' I said, quietly.

Outside it was pouring. People in short flimsy T-shirts were running towards cover. I pulled my jacket up around my neck.

My brother was innocent. I was absolutely sure.

# 4

When I finally called my dad he came straight home from work. I watched out of the living-room window as he parked his car half up on the pavement, got out and slammed the door. His shoulders were rounded as he walked up the path. His face was dark and stormy. I'd seen that look before.

It was early afternoon and in my hand I had a notepad with my **Things To Do** list on it. I'd made it up the previous day. There were various items: shopping (bread and bananas), dry-cleaning (Dad's suit), shoe repairs (Brad), repeat prescription (Dad), book squash court (Dad). At the very end of the list, in big letters, dwarfing everything else, I'd written **Dad To Ring Max Robbins**.

'What time did they come?' my dad said, letting the front door bang behind him.

'Early. About half seven,' I said.

He stood heavily in the hallway, his arms hanging at his sides. His short-sleeved shirt was undone at the neck and the cord of his identity card had twisted round. I could see the passport-sized photograph and the words *Lee Simon, Computer Technician, Insurance Division*.

'Why didn't you ring me?'

19

'Brad didn't want me to.'

'Of course he didn't! Brad never wants me to know anything he's up to. That doesn't mean that you shouldn't ring me.'

My dad's voice was heavy with disappointment. Whether it was with me or Brad I wasn't sure.

'What did they say? What did Brad say?'

'Nothing much. They didn't explain anything, except what I told you about the crash. Brad just went with them.'

My dad made a face. As if to say, *That's it! He's guilty.*

'I saw Mr Haskins down at the station and he said that there were witnesses. It happened yesterday. On the M25. Near the Epping Bridge. I looked it up on the internet . . .'

'You saw Tony Haskins?' my dad said, brushing past me, flinging open the kitchen door. 'What's it going to look like? You're down at the station but his dad's not bothered. You should have rung me!'

'He didn't want me to,' I said, clutching my list.

'I needed to know!'

My dad turned away, opening and shutting the cupboard doors as if he was looking for something. He opened the freezer door and rummaged through the shelves; the sound of frozen food skidding around made me even more anxious.

'Isn't there any bread?' he said, slamming the door and pulling the kettle towards the sink.

'I did what I thought was best,' I said, putting down my pad.

He swung round, looking cross, and then, in a second, his face crumpled.

'Charlie, Charlie . . .' he said, plonking the kettle down in the middle of the kitchen table, 'I'm sorry. None of this is your fault.'

'He couldn't have done what they said. Brad wouldn't throw stones down on to a motorway.'

'Yes, well,' my dad sighed, 'I remember saying that when he first got arrested. *Brad isn't a thief. He's not stupid enough to handle drugs . . .* But it turned out that he was . . .'

'This is different. This is about hurting people. He wouldn't do that.'

'He gets into enough fights.'

'Between him and other lads like him. This is . . . calculated. Brad wouldn't . . .'

'You're right there. Brad never thinks further ahead than the next five minutes.'

We both managed weak smiles. My dad looked like he was going to say something else then changed his mind.

'Do you want me to make you something? A cheese toasted?' I said.

'Go on then,' he answered, as if to say, *You've twisted my arm.*

'I'll get the bread,' I said, reaching into the bread bin, the only thing he hadn't opened.

'I'll ring Max Robbins. He'll tell us what to do. He's a good bloke. He ought to . . .'

My dad opened the kitchen door and stood for a few seconds.

'Put a few slices of tomato on, will you, Charlie? I'll have it in my room. I'll make a couple of phone calls, see if I can find anything out.'

I took my time making the sandwich. I let the grill heat up as I sliced the bread and the cheese and then the tomatoes. It was best to let Dad cool down a bit. His first reaction to Brad's problems was always rage. After a while he was usually calmer. I got some tinfoil out and lined the grill tray. Then I put the bread in to toast. I cleared up, wiping the crumbs away and rinsing off the knife. When it was ready I sprinkled salt on the tomatoes and looked round. The kitchen was tidy. Just how I liked it.

I took the sandwich and knocked lightly on the door of my dad's study. There was music playing low and as I walked in I saw the website for BBC London News was on his PC. I'd been on the site earlier. The *News in Brief* section was on screen: **Motorway Crash Causes Havoc on M25**.

*At 7:05pm yesterday west of junction 26 a car transporter collided with a people carrier and caused a crash which involved eight vehicles. Five members of the public have been injured including a motorbike courier. The driver of the car transporter is being treated for broken ribs and shock. Police sources say that the lack of fatalities was due to light traffic and good driving conditions.*

'Eight vehicles,' my dad said, taking the plate with an air of absent-mindedness.

'It's near High Beech.'

'I know the bridge. I've seen kids up there myself.'

'Did you speak to Max?'

Max Robbins was Brad's probation officer.

'He's not in the office today. I also rang Tony Haskin's mobile. No answer.'

My dad sank his teeth into his sandwich and I cleared away a pile of papers and perched on the edge of his desk. After the first couple of times that Brad got into trouble my dad got to know Tony Haskins. He had arrested Brad for possession of cannabis. He'd been nice, almost apologetic about the arrest and visited our house with details of a drugs counselling programme that Brad could have attended. Since then he'd become a plain clothes detective and been involved in a mobile phone initiative, only to run into Brad again, in possession of a couple of stolen sets. Tony was usually sympathetic. He'd been standing in our kitchen one day and I'd overheard him telling my dad that Brad would grow out of it. *He's a bit of an idiot, if you don't mind me saying. He's like a naughty kid. I don't think he's got a bad bone in his body. Just a load of stupid ones.*

My dad was scrolling down the news to see if there was anything else. An **Update** gave more information:

*The driver of the car transporter has yet to be interviewed by police. Other witnesses have reported a group of people on the motorway footbridge and there are suggestions that a missile was thrown. Police sources say that this aspect of the crash is being taking very seriously and that a number of lines of enquiry are being pursued. Unconfirmed reports suggest that a male, aged nineteen, has been taken in for questioning.*

I pursed my lips. My dad sat back in his chair and ate away at his sandwich, taking giant bites and chewing them with determination. After a while he spoke.

'Oh, I wish Brad would be more like you.'

'Don't say that, Dad.'

I hated it when he started to praise me on the back of Brad's troubles.

'It's true. You've never given me a moment's worry. You're smart and hardworking.'

'Brad's brainy,' I said.

'You're dependable, considerate, easy to get on with.'

'Brad's generous though,' I said. 'And funny.'

'Yeah, well I'm not laughing.'

We both sat in silence for a minute, my dad finishing his food. Dad thought I was some kind of saint. Brad, on the other hand, could never do anything right. Whatever he did Dad wasn't happy. The music was too loud; the CDs were out of their covers; he made too much noise late at night; he left the towels in a heap on the bathroom floor. Even if Brad washed and dried the dishes Dad complained because they weren't put back in their usual places.

The fact was Brad wasn't all bad and I wasn't all good. My halo had definitely slipped over the last couple of weeks and I'd begun to feel this wriggle of guilt whenever Dad praised me. Denny Scott had changed me. It was as if I was deliberately deceiving my dad. There was a new me emerging and I had to keep it a secret from him.

'I keep thinking, you know . . . If your mum were here. Would Brad be different?'

I stared at him. It was an unexpected thing for him to say. If *Mum* were here? My *mother*? He was looking at me as though he wanted an answer and I thought hard for a few seconds but nothing came. Then the front door bell sounded, twice in quick succession.

'Who's that?' I said.

I was glad to turn away and I walked quickly up the hall and opened the door. Brad was standing there, bold as brass.

'I didn't take my keys with me this morning,' he said, walking past me, as if it was a regular day and he was just in from work early.

'What happened?' I said, adding, 'Dad's here.'

He mumbled something.

'I *had* to ring him!' I shrugged.

Then Brad did something odd. He gave me a hug, squeezing my ribs. I could smell tobacco off his clothes and I patted his arm, feeling a blush creeping up my neck. He let go of me and walked along the hall. He paused for a minute then went into Dad's study and stood as far away from his desk as he could. I watched from the door. Dad's face was blank.

'What's happened?' I heard him ask.

'Nothing. They let me go. They had no right to pull me in in the first place,' Brad said, his voice petulant, aggressive even.

'Then why did they?' my dad said, calmly, twisting away from him, touching the mouse and scrolling up the website until the headline was clear: **Motorway Crash Causes Havoc on M25**.

'They were just asking me questions.'

'Why you, though?' my dad said, his chair swivelling back so that he was facing Brad.

'I don't know. Because they've got it in for me?'

My dad nodded, knowingly. I felt my jaw clenching.

'Like everyone else has had it in for you. Your teachers; the people you robbed; the lads you beat up.'

'Lucky for me I've got you on my side.'

Brad's voice was heavy with sarcasm. He and my dad stared at each other, their eyes locked. I shivered. I did not want this to turn into a horrible row. Weren't things bad enough already?

'Do you want something to eat?' I said weakly, grabbing Brad's elbow.

Brad turned to me and gave me a half-smile. He went to say something but changed his mind. He put his hand on my shoulder and I could feel it trembling. He shook his head and I could see him swallowing hard as if he had something stuck in his throat. Then he walked out of the room.

'See what I mean?' my dad said, slumping in his chair. 'Nothing affects him. Me and you, we're all upset and worried but does he care?'

I wasn't so sure about that. I put my hand up to my shoulder where Brad had placed his. That and the hug.

These were not things that Brad usually did. He hated physical contact and loathed it when we had family visitors who insisted on kissing him. I went out into the hall. From above I could hear running water in the bathroom. I raised my foot to go up the stairs then changed my mind. I went into the kitchen and sat down at the table.

There we were. All alone; my dad in one room, me in another and Brad upstairs. It was family life as I knew it.

## 5

Emily came round. Her mum dropped her off about seven.

'I'll be back at ten,' Mrs Little said, giving Emily a peck on the cheek.

Emily gave a backwards wave as she walked into my house. 'Bye, love, Bye, Charlie.'

The door closed and Emily gave a sigh.

'I've had a pig of a day!' she said, 'The printer broke down just when I was downloading stuff on Heroines of Victorian Literature off the internet. Then, when I started boxing up stuff in my room I got dust up my nose and had this attack of sneezing. I think the dust gave me a migraine. Anyway, I thought you were going to come round? I thought we might start on some painting this afternoon.'

'Yeah, well. I haven't had that great a day myself,' I said. 'Come upstairs, we can use my printer.'

I told her all about Brad. She sat cross-legged on my bed while I gave the details. I shaped the story, giving it a bit of drama and emphasizing the fact that it was all a mistake and Brad was innocent. Emily sat quietly while I explained. She was a good listener, letting me speak without interrupting, but a couple of times I saw the faintest hint of disapproval flashing across her face as I spoke. Her eyebrows lifted slightly, her lips pursed for just a second, her fingers fiddled with the bridge of her nose as though she was pushing up some invisible glasses. When I finished there was a moment's silence.

'Um.'

She said it with a great exhalation of breath as if to say, *It doesn't surprise me one bit that Brad's in trouble again!*

We went on line and Googled Charlotte Bronte. There were 112,000 results. Emily scrolled and opened a few up. I let her read on, making little exclamations as she went: *Knew that! Knew that! Blah, blah, blah . . . Already read that!* I ummed and ah'd but really my mind wasn't on it. I was conscious of the other people in the house. My dad downstairs in his study, probably hunched over his computer; Brad in his room, no doubt lying flat out on his bed, his television on, his door tightly shut. How long had it been since the two of them had been able to sit down and have a conversation? Something that didn't spark into an argument. Months.

'You know what?' Emily's voice interrupted my thoughts. 'There are parallels with your family here. The Bronte sisters had an older brother, Branwell. He had a drink problem. He caused Charlotte's family a lot of grief.'

Emily turned back to the computer oblivious to the impact of what she'd just said. No doubt she assumed she was being helpful in some way. I sighed. We'd been friends for years but there were times when I felt a tiny spark of hatred for her.

Emily thought the worst of Brad. She didn't say it but I knew. It stemmed from the early days of our friendship.

She lived nearby then and would often pop in after school. At first she'd been quite impressed by my older brother. She was thirteen and he was sixteen. I even think, for a while, she'd had a bit of a crush on him. She'd offer to make him cups of tea and try to have conversations with him about his football team. He'd been horrible though. When Brad was sixteen he'd treated everyone younger than him with contempt. He called her names behind her back: *Brain of Britain* or *Lady Emily* or *Mummy's Girl* or worse.

At school he'd snub us both, saying that we were boffins and that we sucked up to the teachers. I didn't care. I knew he didn't mean it but Emily would always rise to it. In the end she learned to ignore his remarks, closing her eyes with forbearance if he was rude to her.

'Can't you be nice to her? She's my best friend!' I'd said to him more than once.

'She's always in my face,' he'd replied. 'Posh cow.'

Emily was different from everyone else at school. That's why I liked her. The kids I'd been friends with before seemed to go through a rapid change of personality as soon as we landed at secondary school. Instead of playing games at break or racing about they started to sit in tight little knots talking about lip-gloss and clothes and bras. Some of them started to develop really quickly. Girls the same age as me started to sprout breasts. They didn't want to run round, they wanted to sit and talk about boys and the only game they were interested in playing was kiss chase.

It meant that I spent a lot of time in the library on my own. I got to know the librarian and helped her sort through the tickets and keep the books in order. One day a girl from another form joined me.

'This is Emily Little,' the librarian said. 'Charlotte and Emily. All you need is a friend called Anne and you'd be the Bronte girls!'

Emily gave a brilliant smile at this. She was tall like me and wore small penny glasses. Her hair was long, loose and wavy and she kept it in place with clips. She had the complete uniform with huge black shoes that were weird, a bit embarrassing – even I thought so.

'They're shaped to help feet grow in the natural way,' she said when she saw me looking. 'Modern shoes deform feet. These allow them to breathe.'

She loved reading and so did I. She worked hard and so did I. She had no close friends in her class. Same as me. We began to meet at break and lunch-time. We met a few streets along and walked to and from school together. We spent our free time in each other's houses. In year eight the Head of Year moved us into the same form. Luckily, she stopped wearing the shoes and became a bit more like everyone else. She was forthright though, always giving her views on stuff. The other kids rolled their eyes when she put her hand up in class. I didn't care though. They were the dimwits or *lumpen* as she called them. We were the elite. A year later she and her mum moved but she kept coming to school and I got lifts or buses to her place.

'Was Dennis Scott arrested?' she asked now.

'No!' I said. 'And Brad wasn't *arrested*. He was just called in for questioning!'

Her shoulders twitched as she tapped on the keyboard. Whenever she spoke about Denny she used his full name. Her question made me think of him. I wondered what he was doing at that moment. No doubt he was with Tania Nicholls. I pictured them together, Tania standing on tiptoes, her arms reaching up to him, him scooping her up and taking a rough kiss from her mouth. The thought of it made me feel momentarily sick, light-headed, and I felt a blush creeping up my neck.

'You're miles away,' Emily said.

I coughed. 'I was thinking about decorating. I could come over in the morning. What time do you want me?'

'Anytime,' Emily said. 'You know me, I always get up early.'

I nodded. After a while I went downstairs and got us two glasses of juice. Carrying them up I paused outside Brad's room. I could hear the sound of his television and I was suddenly impatient for Emily to go because I wanted to talk to him to try and smooth it over between him and Dad. When I went back into my room Emily was sitting upright; her shoulders were straight and her head high as though she was balancing a book on it.

'Look at this. Road deaths up by two per cent. Last year 3,508 people were killed on the roads! And here's another local accident; a hit-and-run.'

She pointed to the screen. I gave it my half-hearted attention. I'd had enough information on road traffic accidents for one day.

'It's in our area. A silver car was seen speeding away

33

from an accident involving two children who were waiting at a bus stop, blah, blah, blah, accident black spot, several crashes at this point throughout the previous year, discussions in council regarding a pelican crossing, blah, blah . . .'

She turned round to face me, taking her juice and sniffing at it.

'Um . . . Orange and mango, my favourite.'

Her mum called about ten. My dad opened the door and I could hear him chatting to her, his voice still a little flat after the evening row. Emily picked up all the pages she'd printed off and went ahead of me downstairs.

I glanced round the room. On the computer screen were the road accident statistics she'd been quoting. I walked across and switched it back to the screensaver.

'See you in the morning, about nine?' she said, walking along the hallway towards her mum.

I nodded. Mrs Little was beaming, her eye on Emily's printouts. She gave me a look, a half-rolling of her eyes as if to say, *Look at my clever daughter. All this knowledge she's downloaded!*

'Bye, Charlie,' she said.

They walked off down the path, Emily linking arms with her mum, a babble of girlish chatter coming from the two of them. I envied them. Here I was stuck in a house of men. Even my name *Charlotte* had been too much for everyone.

I was *Charlie*. One of the lads.

# 6

I went upstairs later and tapped lightly on my brother's bedroom door.

'What?'

I opened the door. He was sitting up at his computer amid the usual mess of his room. His clothes lay in piles on his floor and there were silver discs dotted around, CDs and DVDs. Magazines were scattered across the bed and there were plates and dishes perched at angles on the windowsill and on his chest of drawers.

'Dad said Denny phoned a few minutes ago. Your mobile must be off.'

He grunted. 'It's on silent,' he said.

'Do you want anything? Food?'

He shook his head. He had one hand on the mouse and was moving it from side to side. His back was rounded and he looked as though there was a huge load on it.

'It's all right,' I said, 'I know you're innocent.'

He gave a shrug. As if he didn't care what I thought. I left him there and went back to my room.

Without getting undressed I lay back on my bed. I could hear his voice from next door. He was probably talking to Denny on his mobile. Maybe Denny would reassure him, make him feel better. I hoped so.

I rolled over and pushed my face into my pillow. Now that the day's troubles had subsided and Emily had gone home I could relax and let myself think about Denny. I couldn't help thinking about Tania Nicholls too. I'd seen her a few times before but I pictured her as she'd looked standing in the pub car park at High Beech a couple of nights earlier. She had long dark hair that hung in strips around her face. She wore a short, fitted leather jacket and tight skirt with high heels. Brad had told me she worked in a building society. Denny had met her while drawing out some money and they'd been together for about three months.

Through the wall I could hear Brad's voice, low and intermittent. The silences meant that Denny was speaking. What was he saying? Would he ask about me? Would he say, *How's Charlie?* I shook my head foolishly. He wouldn't mention me because he didn't want Brad to know. *Isn't it more exciting? Being secret?* he'd said.

And it was. Secret and exciting. I hadn't even told Emily. I smiled to myself. My best friend thought she knew me. How shocked she would be if she knew what I had been doing. She had lumped Denny in with all my brother's mates, I knew. She would never believe him capable of such feelings, such *passion*. Not that Emily wasn't romantic. She was. She loved all the set texts that had 'love' stories in them. She was always reading poems and sonnets. She loved the idea of Romance. In real life she was less enthusiastic. She simply wasn't interested in lads.

When we were younger it was something that had

pleased me. The constant fascination among my friends for greasy, sweaty boys made me feel mildly nauseous. They were always chewing with their mouths open or burping or farting. They didn't seem able to have a conversation without sliding off into giggles or hoots of derisive laughter. The thought of touching any of them repulsed me. I didn't say any of this to anyone but when Emily and I were placed in the same form and some of the boys started to look at her she said, *Don't they just make you want to become a nun!* I agreed whole-heartedly.

We did talk about romance and sex. We discussed the books we'd read and the films we saw. But it was as if these were things to come, they belonged to the *future* just like uni and careers. They would happen with the right person. They didn't belong to our everyday life. The lads we mixed with were irritants to us not potential boyfriends. It was an unspoken thing between us. Sex and love were on the cards but only in the future. We weren't in any rush.

This had been fine for years. I hadn't felt that I was missing anything. It was like reading about an exotic country. I knew I would travel to it one day but I was in no rush. Emily felt the same. We were virgins by choice.

Emily had had some experience though. She had been to a family party and ended up in a dark corner with the son of a neighbour. She'd told me afterwards that it had been disgusting. *It was like having my face washed by someone's tongue,* she'd said shivering exaggeratedly. She'd dipped her toe in the water and found it unpleasant. She'd done that much.

Before Denny I was completely inexperienced. Brad had

summed me up in a jokey way when his mates had come round one afternoon some months before. A couple of the lads had made flirtatious comments about me and Brad had put his arm around my shoulder protectively and spoke in a pretend-serious voice.

'My sister is an innocent little thing. She's never even been kissed so you scum keep your hands to yourself.'

I'd felt a crimson blush take hold of my throat. I'd glanced around and caught Denny's eye. I had never been kissed, not then.

That changed. One day, four weeks ago, when Denny called round unexpectantly. Brad was out. I was pleased to see him. I liked him a lot. He seemed more mature than my brother. He made me laugh and always took the time to talk to me. When my brother insulted me or had a dig about something Denny always took my side. *Don't treat your little sister like that!* he'd say, grinning at me.

He'd been in the rain and was wet, his hair flattened and the shoulders of his jacket damp.

'The car broke down,' he explained. 'I left it three streets away. I thought Brad would have jump leads.'

I took his jacket and hung it on the chair. He was tugging at his wet hair with his fingers.

'Got a comb?' he said.

'Upstairs,' I said, and skipped out of the kitchen.

In my room I found a clean comb and was about to take it downstairs when I saw he had followed me up. He must have misunderstood me so I handed him the comb and stood sheepishly in the middle of my room, a quick glance around to make sure there was nothing embarrassing lying around.

'All right if I use the mirror?' he said.

'Sure.'

The duvet was a bit crumpled but the rest of the room was neat. He stood by my long mirror bending his knees so that he could see his hair in it.

'It's sticking up at the back a bit,' I said, after he'd combed it for a few moments.

'Do it for me, will you?'

He sat on my bed. It gave me an odd panicky feeling. I took the comb and fussed over his hair, starting with the front. He was only a breath away from me. I could smell the damp from him. I had to stand straight in front, my arms raised, my midriff showing. He moved his hand for some reason and it touched my thigh, sending a thrill through me.

'You could have a ring,' he said suddenly.

I stood back, puzzled.

'In there,' he said, pointing to my midriff. 'In your belly-button.'

I coughed, feeling my face and neck slowly reddening. 'I think it's done,' I said.

'What about the back?' he said, with a half-smile.

I went back to combing. I knew his hair didn't need any more but I let the comb snake through the wet strands. I was close to him, leaning across him. My chest was tingling, my mouth was dry. My T-shirt had risen up again and I could feel the cold air on my belly and at that moment, more than anything, I wanted him to put his hands on my skin.

'Is it true that you've never been kissed?' he said.

I stood back, pulling my T-shirt down, letting the comb drop on to the bed. I was going to say, *No!* I was going to deny it, say, *You know what Brad's like!* But I couldn't. The words would not come out. I felt this surge of emotion inside me, my legs and arms rippling with goose-pimples, my chest hard.

'You've never been kissed, then?' he said, standing up, in front of me, his hands lazily reaching for my waist, drawing me towards him.

I shook my head and lifted my face as he pressed his mouth on mine.

'Open your lips,' he whispered, his fingers gripping my ribs. 'Use your tongue. Like this . . .'

The room went dark for me. It was another country, another world. I reached up and pulled him closer, letting my fingers pull at his wet hair.

That was the beginning.

From then on it felt like a tiny hurricane was blowing through me. I thought about Denny all the time. I tried to be around when he came to call for Brad. At night, in bed, I was restless. I threw off my covers and my nightdress. I lay, naked, in the dark of my room, imagining him there, rubbing my skin against the cool bedclothes, a dull ache taking hold of me.

How could I tell Emily? What was there to tell?

My eyes began to feel heavy and even though I was still dressed I reached out and turned off the bedside light. After a while I must have dozed off.

When I woke up I stared into the darkness of my room. I wasn't thinking of Denny. I was thinking of Brad being taken to the station in a police car. I pictured him in the back seat sitting next to Tony Haskins, Tony telling Brad how disappointed he was in him, maybe brushing his suit down so that he looked smart when he went to court. Then Emily's face popped into my head, disapproval seated on her mouth as I told her the story. Then my dad's voice: *I wish Brad was more like you, Charlie . . .*

I sat up feeling stiff and weary. I turned to the clock. 02:21. I'd been asleep for hours. Without turning the light on I got up and clumsily got out of my clothes. I put my nightie on and went out to the toilet. The lights were off in the hallway and downstairs was dark. My dad was in bed but there was still a glow coming from under Brad's door.

On my way back from the bathroom I wondered if I should knock and try and have another word with Brad. I paused at his door, not able to make up my mind. He might be pleased to see me but it was just as likely that he would be annoyed at my interference. I hesitated. An odd sound was coming from inside his room. I held my breath for a moment trying to work out what it was. It was a sniffing sound.

I pressed my ear to the door, listening for a few moments, waiting for it to stop, but it didn't. He was *crying*. It gave me a sick feeling inside. It was years since I'd seen Brad cry. Not since all the trouble with our mother. In those days he'd cried openly, big watery tears skidding down his face, wiping them away with his knuckles. Then one day it stopped. Nothing made him cry after that. He met his problems with aggression, his jaw squared and his hands clenched in fists. Tears were a thing of the past.

Yet he was crying now. I raised my hand to knock on his door and then stopped. The sound seemed louder for a moment then it died away replaced by a bout of nose blowing. I wanted to go into his room and ask him what was wrong. I hesitated. I couldn't help but think of the police and the accident on the motorway. He'd seemed odd when he came in, embracing me, putting his hand on my shoulder.

I tapped on the door lightly, twice. Then I gave a louder knock.

'Brad? Are you all right,' I said, in a loud whisper.

There was a sound. Brad was moving about.

'Brad?'

He came to the door and opened it a couple of centimetres.

'Are you all—' I started to say.

'I'm just blowing my nose, Charlie. Go to bed. I'm all right.'

'Are you sure . . .?'

The door closed in my face. I stepped back in a huff. My shoulders dropped and I leaned against the wall next to Brad's door. What was happening to everyone? I slid down and sat on the floor, my legs and arms crossed as if I was waiting for someone to come. No one did.

I was completely alone.

After a while I went to bed.

# **Tuesday**

# 7

Paul Sullivan woke up at six o'clock.

'Morning, Paul!' a voice said.

Moments later there was a nurse standing on each side of his bed. One was wrapping a rubber sleeve around his arm and the other was poking an electric thermometer into his ear. For a moment he thought he was dreaming. From somewhere in his head he remembered the accident. Driving along, singing at the top of his voice, then there was darkness, blackness, like he was inside a wooden box. There were sounds as well: the cry of an ambulance, the noise of machinery. Eventually he saw faces; men's faces in yellow hats. They were calling him by his first name. *Are you all right, Paul? Can you speak, Paul? Are you in any pain, Paul?* Had he told them his name was Paul? He must have.

One nurse was well built with a no-nonsense ruddy face. She was holding his wrist, taking his pulse. She was looking at her watch and seemed impatient as if she was willing his heart to pump his blood faster. The other nurse, a young fresh-faced girl, looked like she should be in school uniform. She gave him a reassuring smile. She had braces on her teeth just like his daughter, Danielle.

Josie, his wife, had been there as well, by his bed. He'd opened his eyes a few times and seen her leaning across him. He'd been heavy with sleep, like a deep-sea diver, surfacing from time to time but weighed down by the water and slipping back underneath before he could actually say a word. Maybe even Danielle had come, perched on the end of his bed, saying, *When's Dad going to wake up?*

He suddenly wanted to go home. A powerful need gripped him to be there in his own house, sitting on the curve of an armchair or lying on top of the duvet watching the bedroom telly while Josie vacuumed around him. He would get dressed and go. Just like that. He raised his head to sit up but a feeling of nausea overwhelmed him.

'There, now,' the big nurse said, 'take it easy. You've had something to help you sleep. It'll take a while to wear off.'

The thin nurse was giving him a half-moon smile, her brace shining under the lighting. Or was that his imagination? Paul Sullivan felt himself being sucked down into another sleep. There was no good trying to fight it. He let his eyes close.

Tony Haskins sat in the hospital canteen. His notebook was flat on the table and he'd already ticked off a list of people he'd interviewed about the crash. In front of him was a coffee and a doughnut. He'd only had his breakfast a couple of hours before but still, it was best to take a break while there was time. He'd be run off his feet the rest of the day. Looking up he saw Dominic Kennedy, another CID officer, walking towards him.

'All right, Dom?' Tony said.

Dom pulled out a chair and sat opposite. He placed a bottle of water and an apple on the table between them.

'Do you know how many calories there are in one of those?' Dom said, pointing at the doughnut.

'I need my sugar.'

'Fruit. An apple, an orange, some seeds,' Dom said, straightening his back and moving his elbows back and forward as if he was warming up for a session at the gym.

'You here for the hit-and-run?' Tony said, picking up the doughnut, using his thumb and finger like tongs.

'One dead, the other one in shock,' Dom said.

Tony Haskins shook his head. He was glad he wasn't involved. He'd seen a dead child once before and it had upset him for days.

'I'm waiting to speak to the driver in the motorway crash.'

'M25? Sunday. Kids throwing stones?'

He nodded. Dom's mobile went. He took it out and spoke into it rapidly, pushing back the chair and standing up before the call was finished.

'Got to go. Someone got a better look at the car.'

Tony nodded and watched Dom work his way through the tables towards the exit. He took a bigger bite from his doughnut, holding the saucer underneath to catch the jam. He didn't want to stain his clothes.

At ten-fifteen he walked upstairs to the ward. He headed

for the corner where Paul Sullivan had been the day before. The bed was empty, the covers thrown back as though someone had just got up. Tony Haskins pulled over a chair and sat and waited. At least the man was awake. He looked idly round the ward and glanced at his watch from time to time. It was possible Mr Sullivan was having a shower. Ten minutes later when there was no sign of him something dawned on Tony Haskins. The bedside cabinet had nothing on top of it. He pulled open the door and inside was empty. A male nurse came over and asked him what he was doing.

'I'm here to see Mr Sullivan?' he said.

'He discharged himself. His wife came about half an hour ago. It was against doctor's advice. I don't even think he signed himself out. Heads will roll,' the nurse said, with a knowing look. 'Probably mine.'

Tony Haskins swore under his breath. He'd missed the prime witness. Now he'd have to go round to his house and talk to him there.

# 8

I woke up later than usual. I got dressed quickly and peeped into Brad's room. There was no sign of him, just his duvet halfway on to the floor, mingling with the rest of the mess. I went downstairs and made myself some tea and toast and thought about the crying that I'd heard in the middle of the night. It unsettled me. Something was wrong with Brad. Was it just that he was upset at having been accused of something he hadn't done? I stopped chewing my toast, placed it back on the plate and pushed it away. That sort of thing had never worried him in the past. Brad seemed to accept the police in his life as an occupational hazard.

After a while I picked up my copy of *Jane Eyre* and was just about to leave when I got a text message from Denny. All it said was, *Charlie, thinking of you.* It stopped me dead in my tracks. I leaned on the front door. What did he mean? Did he picture me? My face in a kind of frame, as if I was a photograph he had in his wallet? Or was it an image of me lying dishevelled on the carpet, my jeans undone, my shirt pushed up, my earring long gone?

Looks. They weren't important. That's what Emily thought. People shouldn't be defined by their bodies or faces or the colour of their hair. It was their personalities that counted. Emily refused to wear make-up or put any product in her hair. She also wore plain, unfashionable clothes and flat shoes. The unfair thing was that Emily, in spite of her indifference, had turned out to be pretty in a *girly* way. Her long wavy hair was perfect to plait or pull up on top. Her skin had a rosy hue and her eyebrows gave her a slightly puzzled look. When she took her glasses off she looked nice, attractive. She was shorter than me and a little heavier and she had proper breasts which gave her a shape. And because she thought she was more intellectual than the other kids, she had a kind of snooty look which made her pout. Boys looked at her. Men looked at her in the street. She didn't care though.

Since the thing with Denny I had hung around the mirror more than usual. I felt that I needed to look at myself. What did Denny see when he looked at me? That morning I gazed into the long hall mirror and all I saw was pale skin and flat hair and a long straight body. My eyes were neither big nor small. My face looked average. Turning to the side I saw the slight profile of my breasts. Otherwise someone could have drawn me with a ruler. I was nothing much to look at. Not like Emily.

Sighing, I fluffed my hair with my hand, picked up my keys and left the house.

Emily was organized, all her belongings packed into cardboard boxes. We got started with the decorating as soon as I arrived. We moved her stuff into the hallway and then set about covering the remaining furniture with sheets. The ceiling was high and we both needed ladders.

'You start at that end of the room,' she said, bossily. 'And remember, do it in squares, that way you can remember which bits you've done.'

We worked quietly on, the radio on in the background; a phone-in programme about various things: factory farming, dieting and health. Emily put in an occasional huffed response to a caller but I wasn't really paying attention. I was thinking about Brad and my dad and their rows. Then Tony Haskins come into my head and the awful accident. Then there was Denny, always at the back of my thoughts. Everything was going round in my mind when Emily and I came together in the middle of the ceiling. My neck was sore, my arm aching, and I was squinting trying to work out which sections had already been done.

My mobile rang. I put the roller down in its tray, went to my bag and pulled out my phone. It was my dad.

'I've just heard from Brad. He's at the police station. He's given them a statement saying that he was on the footbridge when that accident happened.'

'No!'

Emily had stopped painting and was standing, holding her roller, looking concerned.

'I'm going down there myself,' my dad said. 'I'm just telling you so you know what's . . . happening.'

There was a lot of interference and I couldn't quite hear him.

'Do you want me to come?' I said, raising my voice as if it was him who couldn't hear me.

'No, I'll see you at home later.'

'Will Brad have to stay at the station?'

'No, they're bailing him. I'll have to go. I'll see you later. No idea what time we'll be back.'

The line went dead. I looked over at Emily.

'What's up?' she said.

I shrugged and sat down on the bed, mucking up the dustsheet that we'd put there.

'Is it Brad?'

I nodded. Her face was blank. I told her what had happened.

'But yesterday . . .'

'He said he wasn't there!'

'So he caused the accident . . .'

'No, not necessarily.'

'But if he threw a stone at a lorry . . .'

'We don't know that. It may have been an accident!'

It was a ridiculous thing for me to say. Emily didn't answer but her jaw looked tightly set as though she was stopping herself from speaking.

'I don't know his side of the story yet,' I went on, 'I need to talk to him. I thought there was something funny, yesterday. In the way he was acting. I could tell he was a bit upset.'

Emily's mouth twisted ever so slightly as if to say, *It isn't possible for Brad to be upset!*

'In the middle of the night I heard him crying.'

I hadn't meant to give Emily this information. Her dislike for my brother meant that I hardly ever talked about him with her.

'Crying?' she said. She looked as though she was on the brink of laughing. I stood up. She was my best friend and I didn't want to fall out with her but I wasn't going to give her the chance to have a go at Brad.

'I'd better go. I'll ring you later and tell you what's happened.'

I pulled off the old shirt I was wearing for the decorating and got my stuff together.

'Do you want my mum to give you a lift home? Shall I come with you?' she said, her voice softer.

I shook my head. Before I left I took a look in her bedroom mirror. My hair was dotted with white paint.

'Do you want some white spirit to get that off?' she said, her own hair cascading from a ponytail at the top of her head, not a spot on it.

I shook my head and left. What does it matter how I look? I thought, taking quick steps down the stairs towards the door.

# 9

I made some sandwiches and covered them with clingfilm, then I cleared up the crumbs and busied myself in the kitchen. I was apprehensive, not knowing what to think. I'd already been upstairs to my room and logged on to the News 24 website. The report had been updated. As far as I knew there were injuries, a couple were said to be serious. Cars had been damaged. What did it mean for Brad? Why had he lied to us?

It was past four in the afternoon before I heard the front door open. There was a mumble of words, not the usual clashing comments and raised voices. I stood for a moment looking at the lunch I'd set out neatly on the table. I clicked the kettle on. Then I heard footsteps going upstairs. My dad's face appeared at the kitchen door. He looked tired.

'Hi, love. We're back. I'm off to try Max Robbins again.'

'I made some food,' I said.

'We got some sandwiches from a bakery.'

'Oh.'

'Pop this lot in the fridge,' he said, turning away. 'We'll have them later.'

'Aren't you going to tell me what happened?'

'Why don't you try speaking to him?' he said, pointing up to the ceiling.

And I was on my own again. I looked at the plates and cups and found myself almost tearful. After taking a few bites of my sandwich I threw it away. I heard a beep and picked up my mobile. It was a message from Emily. *Hope all is well. Want me to come round?* I shook my head as though she was there in the room with me.

A while later I went upstairs.

Brad was lying on his bed holding the remote. He'd drawn the blind down and his room was darkish. He moved his feet so that I could sit on the bed. Then he lowered the sound.

'I thought you said you weren't on that footbridge,' I said.

'Don't start, Charlie,' he shrugged.

'You stood downstairs and you said—'

'I didn't actually say I wasn't there.'

'But you let us believe . . . Me and dad . . .'

'Listen to yourself, Charlie. You sound like my teacher. No, worse, you sound like *him*.'

'Don't say *him* like that. He's our dad!'

I felt my throat cracking up. I swallowed a couple of times in quick succession. I did not want to cry.

'I was there, on the bridge, but I didn't throw the stone, right? There were four of us. We were larking about. Nobody meant to throw a stone. A couple of the lads were throwing them at each other. One of them threw too hard and it just went down on to the road. It wasn't me but I was there.'

'Did you tell that to the police?' I said.

'Why d'you think I've been there all morning!'

'And nobody actually threw it?'

I said it with a kind of wonder in my voice. I remembered the expression on Emily's face when I said that it might have been an accident. Incredulity, disdain. She would always think the worst of Brad.

'Have the police interviewed the others?'

He shook his head.

'Why not?'

'It's not up to me to give information to the police.'

'You haven't told them?'

'I don't grass on my mates, Charlie.'

'But you'll take the blame!'

'A couple of people got injured, right? A few cars got trashed. It was an accident. Nobody meant it to happen. I've got to go back and see them in a couple of days. If they charge me at all it'll be with Criminal Damage. Even though I never actually threw the stone. Like I said, no one threw it. It fell.'

'So why don't the others come forward?'

'Why should they? I wouldn't have come forward only some copper saw my car parked in the forest, near the footbridge. He took my registration.' He shrugged.

'Who else was there?'

'I'm not saying! It doesn't matter anyway. It'll be all over in a couple of days. I'll get a fine.'

'And a police record!'

'I've already got a police record.'

'Was Denny there?'

The thought came to me suddenly. Denny must have been there. Denny and Brad spent all their free time together.

'I'm not saying. I'm not talking about who was there and who wasn't.'

I stood up, agitated. That was it! Brad was protecting Denny.

'Did Denny throw the stone?'

'Nobody *threw* a stone. It dropped. It was an accident and anyway I never said Denny was there.'

Brad sat forward, swinging his legs off the bed. His words were loud.

'You're covering up for Denny!'

'I am not! I'm not saying any more. It's my business, Charlie. Don't go on at me. I've had enough of that from him!' He pointed downstairs. '*Pull yourself together, Brad. Why can't you be more like Charlie . . .?*'

He used a silly voice and it annoyed me.

'Don't have a go at Dad. You're the one who's in trouble!'

'Leave me alone,' he said, cold all of a sudden. 'You're not in charge of me. You're not Mum!'

I stood and stared at him for a moment. He'd thrown *Mum* at me, like scoring a point. After everything that had happened. How could he? He seemed to sense the tension and he looked up at me. Our eyes met.

'I meant . . . I meant, you're not my parent . . .'

'I know what you meant,' I said and walked out of the door.

Later, I went downstairs and into the kitchen and found my dad eating his sandwich.

'Has he told you about the stone falling by accident?' he said, between mouthfuls.

I nodded.

'It's a interesting story but it won't do him any good.'

'How come?' I said, grudgingly, not really wanting to talk about it any more.

'A stone would have to be thrown with great force in order to shatter the windscreen of a lorry. That's why it was called a *missile*. The speed gives it power. Falling stones don't shatter windscreens. If that's Brad's only defence then I'm afraid he's in a lot of trouble.'

'But no one's dead,' I said.

'Three people have got injuries. Four, including the driver. Not to mention the mental trauma of being in such an accident. Then there's the damage to the vehicles and the road. The fact that no one's dead is just good luck. I'm telling you, Charlie. He could go to prison for this. Maybe, it's what he needs.'

'Don't say that.'

My words were half-hearted though. Brad had lied. That was all it boiled down to. That was what the tears were about. Brad facing up to being in trouble again. I opened the fridge. His sandwich was sitting there, tightly covered in clingflim. I took the plate out and threw it into the pedal bin.

A while later he came downstairs. The kitchen door opened and he stood there.

'I thought there might be something to eat,' he said,
sheepishly.

'Make it yourself,' I said.

# 10

At about seven Emily rang. She was on the phone for ages. I took the receiver up to my room. On my bed there was a photograph and I was toying with it while listening to her. A picture of Denny and Brad that I had taken from Brad's room some weeks before. It was a holiday snap from the previous summer. The two of them together. Best friends. I'd looked at it a lot over the last few weeks, feeding my eyes with Denny's face.

Emily asked me about the *Brad situation* and listened in silence to my weary explanation. She then described the rest of her day to me. I listened with half an ear. She'd been on the net looking for blinds and a chest of drawers. IKEA, it turned out, had everything she needed and she wondered if I'd go with her and her mum later in the week. I agreed just to please her. I ended the call and looked at the photograph again. Had Denny been there on that footbridge with Brad? Had he thrown the stone?

I'd heard Brad showering a while before. Unusually there was no music playing, just the sound of the water running. He seemed to be there for an age. I hovered between my room and the upstairs landing. I wanted to talk to him, to *make* him see that he was wrong. When the bathroom door opened he saw me and gave a scowl. I swallowed all my words and went back into my room. Then, moments later, I heard his door open and close and the rattle of his keys. He'd hardly had time to get dressed and now he was going out.

I followed him downstairs and he turned and looked at me with irritation.

'Are you seeing Denny?' I said.

He shook his head.

'How come?' I said. 'Is he seeing Tania?'

'How should I know? I don't know what he's doing. If you're so interested why don't you ask him?'

I felt a blush creeping up my neck and tensed as the front door slammed. Where was he going? Was he even allowed to go out? Would the police be annoyed?

I went back to my room feeling as though I was going to burst with frustration. Then I made a decision. I would go and see Denny. Whatever Brad said, he and Denny were close. If Brad was on that bridge then maybe Denny had been there as well.

I got changed, taking a bit more care than usual. I put some blusher on. I pulled out a shirt and a shortish denim skirt. I intended to go round to Denny's as if I was looking for Brad. Then if Tania was there I wouldn't look silly. If she wasn't then I could talk to Den. I was going for a serious reason. Deep inside me though there was a tickle of excitement at just the thought of seeing him. I left home about half eight, got a bus and then walked from the high road to the street where he lived.

I'd been past Denny's house a few times in Brad's car. I'd sat in the passenger seat as Brad had dropped something off or picked Denny up in order to go out somewhere. In the past it had just been a run-of-the-mill thing to do. This was the first time I had ever come to his house alone. Walking smartly along his street I felt this great bubble of apprehension inside me. Would he be in? Would he be alone? What would he say when he saw me?

And then I felt guilty. I was mixing all my own personal feelings up with my concern for my brother. I was there to find something out. Yet I was also there to see Denny. My motives were all over the place. I slowed down, my steps becoming uncertain. When I was about five houses away I almost stopped and turned away but then I heard a loud female voice coming from the direction of Denny's house. I walked on, clinging close to garden hedges and walls. A row was going on, maybe even some crying, I couldn't quite tell. Then there was the sound of a door slamming. I held my breath as someone burst out of Denny's garden path and walked off in the opposite direction.

It was Tania. I could tell by the long dark hair which hung in strands over her shoulders. I waited for a few moments as she got further away and then turned a corner. Then I walked up to Denny's front door and rang the bell. It opened smartly as if he'd only been a couple of steps away. His face was guarded as if to say, *What do you want, Tania?* but his expression immediately softened when he saw it was me.

'Charlie?' he said.

'I need to talk to you. About Brad. It's important.'

'Right,' he said, stepping back, holding the door open.

I stepped inside. From behind the living-room door I could hear the sound of a television programme. I stood awkwardly, my hands pulling down my denim skirt which suddenly seemed much too short. Denny started to walk in the direction of the kitchen and then changed his mind.

'Come upstairs,' he said, lowering his voice.

I swallowed a couple of times and followed him up the stairs, along the hallway and into his bedroom. I stood uncertainly at the door as he went ahead of me and sat down on a desk chair next to a computer.

'Grab a seat.'

Denny gestured towards a low bed, neatly made, the duvet squarely placed, its edges at right angles, the surface of it smooth. I hesitated, not wanting to untidy it. He took my reluctance for something else.

'Don't worry, Charlie. I'm not going to jump on you!' he said, smiling.

I felt my neck begin to redden and stood where I was.

'Were you with Brad on Sunday night? After you left my house?' I said, breathily, rubbing at my neck to hide the blush.

Denny looked puzzled. His eyebrows tensed for a moment and he didn't answer. My heart sank in my chest. *He was with Brad. He was there on the bridge.*

'Where? What do you mean?' he said.

'On the footbridge? You were with Brad when someone threw the stone at that lorry.'

He shook his head and a smile came on his lips.

'I wasn't there. Brad and me don't do everything together.'

I didn't believe him.

'Brad's going to take the blame. There were four people on the footbridge and Brad's the only one who's been charged. That's not fair.'

Denny stood up, walked across to me and took my arm, pulling me towards his bed. I let myself go. He sat down and I stumbled after him, sitting beside him, shifting a little to put some space between us. He leaned forward on his knees.

'My brother could go to prison,' I said.

'He won't. It was just a bit of vandalism. A few cars got trashed. The police can't prove that Brad threw the stone. He'll get some community time. He'll have to pick up litter along the side of the motorway for a few weeks.'

I frowned. He was talking about it as though it didn't matter.

'People got hurt!' I said.

'No one meant for that to happen. It was an accident. It's just a shame that someone saw Brad's car.'

I didn't know what to say. Denny made it sound so simple.

'Who else was there?'

He turned to me and sighed, a mischievous smile on his face. I'd seen that look many times. It made something tiny flip over inside my chest. He put his hand out and laid it on my shoulder.

'I don't know. I wasn't there,' he said, making little circles with his fingers.

I ignored what he was doing and looked around the room. It was tidy. The drawers closed, no clothes hanging over the backs of chairs. Books and CDs piled neatly on shelves. Everything about him was so orderly, so different to my brother. And yet they hung around together. *Thick as thieves*, my dad had said. I stared ahead as I felt him edge along the bed so that there was no space between us. He placed his hand on the back of my neck and I felt my skin rise up to meet it.

'I'll bet David Morris was there,' I said, mentioning another lad that Brad was friends with. 'And Pete Long. And maybe Desmond Black.'

He used his other hand to pull me towards him so that we were facing each other.

'I don't know for certain who was there,' he said, softly, 'because I wasn't.'

His hand dropped down to my breast. I took a shallow breath and felt myself turn to jelly. His other hand began to undo my buttons. I swallowed, trying not to react to what he was doing.

'And Billy Warner,' I whispered, looking straight into his eyes.

His lashes flickered and he stiffened for a moment. He lifted his hand up to my face. *That was it. Billy Warner had been there. Denny knew because he had been there as well.*

'I don't know,' he said, his voice husky.

He pulled me towards him and kissed me on the mouth, his lips pressing hard on to mine, his arms folding round me, holding me in a vice-like grip. My head went blank and I sank into him, feeling myself falling sideways on to the neat duvet. My shirt was open and he edged on top of me, his face twisting and turning so that the kiss seemed to be never-ending. I half opened my eyes. My chest and legs felt as though they were on fire.

'Denny!'

A voice broke into the room. He stopped abruptly and looked up. There were footsteps coming up the stairs. In a second he rolled off me, stood up and walked across the room to turn a key in the door just as someone was outside.

'What, Mum? I'm just getting changed,' he said, testily.

'I've got your mobile. It's making beeping sounds. It's probably a few sorries from Tania.'

'Could you leave it on the floor? I'll get it when I'm dressed.'

There was some mumbling and then the sound of footsteps back down the stairs. Denny opened the door and picked the mobile up. He looked at the screen and his mouth pursed.

'I'd better go,' I said, standing up, straightening my clothes.

'You don't have to,' he said brightly, putting down his mobile on top of his chest of drawers.

I was doing my buttons up and he walked towards me.

'Let me help,' he said, starting from the bottom and undoing them again.

'Denny!' I said, in a shocked voice.

He kissed me again, slowly, his fingers trailing across the fabric of my shirt. Then his mouth moved to my ear.

'You're so innocent,' he said. 'That's what's so *nice.*'

'Billy Warner?' I said, stepping back, away from him, searching his face for a straight answer.

'Just a short lesson today,' he said, ignoring my comment.

He was my teacher and I was his pupil.

On the journey home I felt guilty. I'd gone to his house for one thing and ended up with something else. The name *Billy Warner* was in my head but I didn't really know if he had been there. I sat on the bus and felt my chest hardening and my throat dry with desire. Did I really care who was on that footbridge? No one else seemed to.

I remembered that Tania had walked out on him and I felt myself perk up. Maybe they would split up. Then there might be a chance for me. Denny and Charlie. Why not? It made me walk with purpose along the streets, a tune in my head, my blood still pulsing with the memory of his hands on my skin.

Indoors I saw my dad sitting on the bottom stair. My mood plummeted. He looked upset. In his hand was his mobile phone.

'What's the matter?' I said. 'Where's Brad?'

'He's still out. I've just had a phone call from Tony Haskins.'

'What's wrong?' I said.

My dad shook his head.

'What's happened?' I said, impatiently.

'That man who was driving the lorry? In the crash?'

I nodded.

'He's dead.'

'Dead?' I said.

'That's right. Your brother's managed to kill somebody.'

# Wednesday

# 11

Josie Sullivan stood looking at the chair that Paul, her husband, usually sat in to watch television. It was green leather and it bore the imprint of Paul's back. He loved that chair. When he got back from three or four days driving over the continent he headed to it, grabbed the remote and waited for her to bring him a drink.

'Life doesn't get much better than this,' he'd say, winking at her, clicking the remote so that the channels fled by.

Sometimes it was a meal that she'd cooked which sat on his lap. Other times it was a pizza or takeaway Indian. The previous day, when he'd got back from the hospital he hadn't wanted a thing.

'A thin piece of toast?' she'd offered.

'A bowl of ice cream,' she'd suggested.

'A milk-shake?' she'd said, her voice dropping, seeing that he wasn't interested.

She'd made herself busy. Danielle had sat on the sofa and watched television with her dad. Josie listened from the kitchen hoping to hear some conversation. She walked in once or twice but all she got was a sleepy smile from Paul.

It was the drugs, she knew. Strong painkillers took days to get out of a person's system. Her main worry was the pain that Paul would feel from his cracked ribs and the bruises when the drugs wore off.

He had been carried away from the crash in a daze, the policeman had said, in a state of shock. When she saw him in A and E she feared the worst. He looked pale and his face was in a grimace and he was holding his chest. It was his heart, she thought, or his lungs had collapsed under the steering wheel. It happened to drivers. No amount of air bags or seat belts could stop the tons of metal that would be pushed back on to the driver in a crash.

Yet Paul's injuries were minor. Broken ribs, very painful but he would recover.

The doctor at the hospital seemed brusque, as if he blamed Paul for the accident. But it hadn't been Paul's fault. Somebody had thrown a stone at his windscreen. Some young man had stood, on the footbridge, and waited until the lorry got close enough and then aimed. Had he watched the crash? Or run off, terrified of what he'd done?

It was beyond understanding.

Josie sat down now in Paul's chair. She felt small, dwarfed by the chunky arms and high back. The leather was smooth and cold.

Paul had been watching something when he'd cried out. A pain in his chest, he'd said. She thought the drugs were finally wearing off. That's how stupid she had been. It was the cracked ribs, she said, bustling round in a no-nonsense way like some busy matron.

It had been a blood clot. He died on the way to hospital. The paramedic had been calm and had used his hands to pump at Paul's chest. He'd said, *Now come on, Paul, my man, come on!* But she'd known. She'd seen the expression on Paul's face. She'd felt his life slip away, brushing past her, out into the surrounding streets. She'd known.

Josie pushed the back of her head into the leather. At least Danielle hadn't been there. She had that to be thankful for. But not much else. A boy throwing stones had ended everything for her. Where was he now? Playing on his computer? Sending messages on his mobile? Tucking into a cooked breakfast?

The sound of the letterbox made her sit forward. The post. She pushed herself up and walked to the front door, her feet heavy in her slippers. She picked up the letters and flicked through. Most of them were for Paul. The bottom one was thick and had the words *Tickets: Open Immediately.*

'What is it, Mum?'

Danielle's voice was tiny. It squeaked at her from the stairs. Josie tried to compose herself before she turned round. She coughed.

'It's the tickets for Portugal,' she said, her eyes swimming with tears.

# 12

When Brad came downstairs the next morning he was smartly dressed. He and Dad were going to see a solicitor; then back to the police station.

Brad was quiet, moving round the kitchen in a stiff and awkward way; pouring his cereal and taking a moment to refasten the packet; getting the milk out and rinsing the plastic bottle before putting it into the pedal bin. He leaned against the worktop to eat and his eyes settled on me, sitting at the table watching him.

'*Don't* say anything, Charlie,' he said, concentrating on what he was eating.

I had no intention of speaking. The conversation I'd had with him the previous evening had not gone well. I'd told him that I knew Denny and Billy Warner had been part of it. He'd told me to mind my own business. I threatened to go the police myself and he lost his temper; took me by the shoulder and shoved me out of his room. I stood outside his door and felt as if I would burst with irritation. Why was he taking the blame? Surely now that it was so much more serious he could see the sense in being truthful? Unless he *had* thrown the stone. Unless *he was guilty*. A man was dead!

His door had stayed shut and I'd gone to my room in a huff.

The truth was that I had nothing to say to my brother. I watched as he scooped up a spoonful of cereal and put it into his mouth. He chewed doggedly as if he really didn't want the food at all.

My dad came into the kitchen.

'I might as well mention this while you're both together,' he said.

Brad turned to him, his spoon in midair.

'I phoned your mother early this morning. I felt . . . I felt she needed to know.'

'Why?' I said, genuinely surprised.

'Because this is . . . could be . . . No, it *is* very serious. She has a right to know.'

'She has no rights,' I said, looking across at Brad, searching his eyes out. We may have fallen out with each other but we were together on this?

'I just thought she should know. It could end up all over the papers anyway.'

Brad didn't answer. He finished his food and put his bowl by the sink. Then he began pushing his palm against his knuckles. The sound of his bones cracking made me soften towards him. Poor Brad. He seemed drawn to trouble, sucked towards it. I got up and walked across and hugged one of his arms.

'Ring me,' I said.

He nodded and then walked towards the door. My dad gave me a look as if to say, *Here we go again!*

But this wasn't the same as all the other times. Someone was dead and Brad was taking the blame.

An hour later Emily was at the front door. She waved to her mum's car as it drove off and then walked past me into my house.

'I only heard about it on the news this morning. I came straight away. I should have rung, probably, but I . . .'

I nodded and she gave me a hug. All of a sudden I went a bit weak. The whole thing was out of control. It was as if me, my dad and Brad were being dragged along by some speeding train.

'It'll be all right,' she said.

'Come into the kitchen,' I croaked.

I made her some tea and told her everything I knew.

'So Billy Warner might have been there?' she said.

'Possibly,' I said, picturing Denny's expression as I said Billy's name.

'Billy Warner. Why should that surprise anyone? Ten to one he threw the stone.'

Billy Warner was one of Brad's old school-friends. We knew him. Most people who went to our school knew him. He was constantly in trouble, standing outside classroom doors, wandering the playground making faces at the classroom windows. At lunch-time he smoked dope and drank cans of cider outside the school fence. He did it in full view as if he wanted to be caught. He spent a lot of time excluded. He had a loud mother who was always up at the school complaining about her son's treatment. Mrs

Warner was famous for screaming at the head teacher across the dining hall.

In Brad's last year at school Billy Warner learned to drive and turned up at our house in a car that looked like it had been sellotaped together. All the trouble in school now transferred itself to the roads and Billy was pulled up for driving without a licence and insurance. Then, even after he'd passed his test, he was pulled up for drink driving, for using a mobile while driving, for driving without tax and insurance. The last I'd heard was that he'd been disqualified for a year.

'We should go and see him,' Emily said. 'He lives on the Waterways estate. I know the house.'

Emily had lived on the Waterways when I first knew her.

'Let's see what he's got to say.'

She was sounding organized and efficient. Why not? I thought. It was a way to pass the time if nothing else.

Billy Warner's house was in a cul-de-sac and as we rang on the bell a delivery lorry pulled up at a house opposite. On the side were the words, SOFA SO GOOD.

'Yes?'

Mrs Warner stood at the door looking past us at the lorry across the way. She was a small woman dressed all in denim with jet black hair and a stud in her nose. Emily seemed to take a step back.

'Mrs Warner?' she said in her nicest voice. 'We're friends of Billy's from school. We were wondering if we could have a word with him?'

'I don't know you,' she said, her voice booming. Her nails were long and had checks on them, like a draughts board.

'I'm Brad Simon's sister,' I said.

'Yeah, I know you,' she said pointing at me, her eyes sliding off to the delivery van.

'Is Billy in?' I said, trying to focus. I turned and watched as two men pulled the back of the lorry down.

'That's the second sofa she's had delivered in the past week,' Mrs Warner said, her mouth rippling.

'Mrs Warner, may we speak to Billy?' Emily said, rounding her words.

Mrs Warner looked at Emily with suspicion.

'What's this about?'

I spoke quickly. 'Brad has given me a message for Billy.'

Mrs Warner took a step past us and stared at the two men who were carrying a giant white sofa out of the back of the van. It was covered in plastic and they were grunting at it.

'I've got a few messages for him as well. If you see him tell him I want him.'

'He's not here?' Emily said.

'Haven't seen him since the weekend. That's not unusual though,' she said with a sigh. 'He comes and goes as he pleases.'

A woman had appeared at the house across the road. She was standing with her arms folded, looking pleased with herself as the delivery men carried her sofa up the path. Mrs Warner let out a *humph* sound.

'Do you have his mobile number?' Emily said, politely.

'Your brother will have his mobile number. Why doesn't he ring him?'

Without another word she slammed the front door. Emily huffed and we began to walk away. Behind us we could hear one of the delivery men's voice, sounding a bit stressed, *To the right, just edge it, to the left, careful . . .*

It had been a silly idea. We didn't even know for certain that Billy Warner had been there on Sunday. And if he had? What would we have said?

'It was worth a try,' I said.

'Horrible woman,' Emily said. 'That's why me and Mum moved away from here. People like her!'

When we got back to my house the answerphone light was flashing. I pressed the button and heard a voice that I hadn't heard for along time.

*'This is a message for Lee, Bradley or Charlotte. It's Sally here. I need to have a talk about Brad. I'll come over. About five-thirty. After Paul's got home from work. I can use the car then.'*

The call ended. I just stood silently, looking stupidly at the telephone.

'Who's that?' Emily said.

'My mother.'

'I thought you said your mother was dead!'

'She is to me,' I said, testily, pressing the 'end' button.

# 13

After Emily had gone home I went up to my room and put some music on. I lay on my bed and thought of the things I had told her about my mother. It had been quite a dramatic day for Emily. She'd been involved in my brother's troubles and she'd heard all the facts about my mum and dad's marriage break-up. She took it well. She didn't dwell on the fact that I hadn't told her the truth. She looked genuinely puzzled and concerned and when her mum called for her she gave me the second hug of the day.

'You meant that she was *metaphorically* dead,' she whispered dramatically and followed her mum out to her car.

I pictured her sitting in the passenger seat and relating my problems. *Charlie's mum left her when she was five. She ran off with Charlie's uncle!* It made me squirm to think of Mrs Little's reaction.

For me though it wasn't a story, it was just an ending. It had all happened over ten years before and I had memories but they were just scraps. I was five years old when she left. In my head were a series of blurred pictures and old images of photographs that I had looked at for a few years.

My mother, Sally, was tall and thin like me. Unlike me she was pretty with long wavy hair that she often used to wear in a plait. Often she let it hang loose, tumbling across one shoulder. She'd never had it cut, she said, not once. The ends of it were thin and fluffy. Her baby hair. When I sat on her lap it used to tickle my face.

She played with me and Brad a lot, building dens, constructing Lego towns and helping us make vegetable gardens. She let us cook and paint and make models of things. She encouraged us to dress up and put on shows for our dad and she played the guitar and sang songs. I only remember it in fragments. She sat by the bay window, her hair snaking across her shoulder, touching the strings of the guitar. Sometimes Paul was there too. He was my dad's younger brother, his long hair tied back in a ponytail. I saw them singing together, I'm sure I did.

And then one day she was gone.

Brad and I sat in his bedroom, our backs against the door, listening to my dad raging on the telephone, shouting at people who came to see him. We watched as he dragged black plastic bags of her things down the stairs. I didn't know what was happening. I just breathed in the hurt in the air, the grief of her absence. Brad knew. He was eight and he understood and became a sort of parent to me. When my real dad was having tantrums and sulks my brother heated up tins of beans and sausages and we played I spy while we were eating. If I asked him about Mum he just said, *She's gone away for a little while.*

We saw her a couple of times at other people's houses.

My dad dressed us up and deposited us at an aunt's house or his mum's while he sat in the car. When my mother came into the room she spent ages hugging us and looking us over, as though she hadn't seen us for years. She looked thinner, light as a feather. I could feel her elbow bones and her ribs when she cuddled me. She seemed to have a cold all the time, sneezing, coughing, blowing her nose. She had a sore on her mouth one day and said she couldn't kiss us. Once when we'd been there for a while I looked out of the front room window and saw Dad sitting in his car. He seemed to have his hands ready on the steering wheel, as though he was a getaway driver. His face looked puffed up, ready to burst, his eyebrows heavy.

On those nights, I always wanted to sleep in Brad's bed. He said no over and over but I crept in beside him anyway.

We stopped seeing her. She went to live in Australia, Dad said, and she was going to write and phone and when we were a bit older we could go on an aeroplane and see her. We got short and cheerful letters every few weeks. We got birthday cards and presents at Christmas. We didn't get the phone calls though. We never heard her speak to us from the other side of the world. After a while, years maybe, the letters stopped and it was just the occasional card.

In my head my mother drifted into some kind of neverland. Most of the time I forgot about her. It was me and Brad and Dad. We did everything together. When I did think of her she was like this fairy princess, her hair tumbling down around her face, her long fingers pulling the strings of a harp. She was hazy though and sometimes she looked like a film star or a cartoon picture from one of my storybooks. I used to think of her as Mummy Who Lived in Australia and one day I would go and see her.

Most of the time though I didn't think about her at all.

The front door banged and shook me out of my reverie. 'Dad?' I called. 'Brad?'

'It's me, Charlie. Brad's still at the police station.'

I got off my bed and walked out to the hallway as Dad pressed the answerphone button. I stood as my mother's message played over. My dad looked up at me, his eyes grating on mine for a second as my mother's voice sounded. When it stopped he cleared his throat and looked at his watch.

'Why didn't Brad come home?' I said. 'Did you see a solicitor?'

My dad mumbled something and walked down the hall towards the kitchen. I ran down the stairs and followed him.

'Where's Brad?' I said.

My dad had his back to me. He was standing at the sink filling a glass with water. He drank it down and then turned.

'They're going to charge him with Manslaughter.'

*Manslaughter.* The word made me stiffen. It had always been a possibility but just saying it out loud made me think of wars and executions. Not a few lads playing about on a bridge.

'Of course Brad won't add anything to his present

statement. He just says *No comment*. His solicitor's due there about three. He'll talk to him and then, if he wants to continue with his story, they'll charge him.'

'What do you mean *story*? Don't you believe him?'

'To be perfectly honest with you, Charlie, I don't know. I've believed him in the past and look where that got me.'

'You think he threw a stone at that lorry?'

Dad looked like he might say yes. My face must have dropped because he seemed to pull himself together.

'I don't know. I just can't tell with Brad any more. Maybe your mum will know.'

'*Mum?*' I said. 'Why should she know anything? What's it got to do with her? It's got nothing to do with her!'

'I know how you feel,' he started, 'but this is a crisis. Your mum might be able to help . . .'

'How? I don't want to see her. Neither does Brad.'

My dad seemed to shrink a little at my words.

'Why don't you go over to your friend's house when Mum comes. I'll see what she has to say. Then you can make your own mind up.'

'I don't want her *here*,' I said, my voice cracking. 'In our house.'

'Charlie, Brad will most certainly go to prison for this, for a long time. I can't deal with this on my own. Your mother has a right to be involved.'

I turned and walked down the hallway. My jacket was over the banister and I grabbed it. The money in my pocket rattled and I could feel the weight of my mobile phone. I picked my keys up by the front door. It was only three in the afternoon but I didn't want to be in the house any longer. Not if my mother was visiting.

Not even to help Brad out.

# 14

I sent Denny a text.

*Can I meet you after work? Important. Charlie.*

He replied, moments later.

*At home. On my own. Sickie. Come round. Denny.*

I rang the bell and he answered immediately. He looked tousled, as though he'd been lying down. He had a shirt over some shorts, looking like he'd just pulled any old clothes on. His face broke into a lazy smile.

'Are you really sick?' I asked.

'Sick of work,' he said, holding the door open. 'Come in. I was just going to have a drink.'

I leaned against the kitchen door while Denny opened the fridge and got out a bottle of Coke. He poured two glasses.

'You're becoming quite a regular visitor, now,' he said, still with his back to me.

'They're charging Brad with Manslaughter,' I said.

He didn't speak

'He'll go to prison. For years maybe,' I said.

He turned. He looked tired. He scratched the back of his head with his fingers.

'He'll take the blame for everyone else. It's not fair, Denny,' I said, my hands together, my fingers knotted.

He shook his head. 'Let's go upstairs,' he said.

I followed him. In his room I sat on a chair opposite his bed. He offered me a drink but I shook my head. He sat on the bed, both drinks on the floor by his foot. The room was in shadow and it seemed like it was evening when it was only late afternoon.

'They won't be able to prove anything. If Brad keeps quiet the case will be thrown out of court for lack of evidence.'

'He's already said he was guilty.'

'No, he said he was there, on the bridge. He was one of the lads. He never said he threw anything. The police have charged him in the hope that the court will see his silence as guilt.'

'They will, won't they?' I said, uncertainly.

'The charges won't hold. If he says that he didn't throw that stone then no one can prove that he did. If you go round asking the other people to own up then who knows what will happen? The person who did throw the stone might put the blame on to Brad and he might end up going to prison. It's better like this. It's better that the magistrates or the jury – whatever – see him as a bloke who's not going to grass his mates up. That makes him look good, loyal. If they see four young blokes in the dock each blaming the other they all look guilty.'

'You were there, weren't you?' I said, sensing something from him.

He shook his head.

'On my mother's life, I wasn't there.'

I searched out his eyes but it was too gloomy in the room for me to see.

'Come here,' he whispered.

I went across and sat beside him.

'It will be all right. Brad will go to court and he might get a smack on the wrist for being there but no one can say that he *did* it. If anything he'll look like the kid who's carrying the can for everyone else and that'll get him sympathy. You've got to stop worrying away at this. Let him do it his own way. He's a man now. You've got to let him make his own decisions.'

It began to make some sense. Denny's voice was soft and silky and I felt like sinking into his words. He put his hand on my neck. His fingers were cool and he moved them in circles. I turned to him and he kissed me, softly for once, his lips just tickling mine. Maybe he was right. Maybe for once my brother knew what he was doing. I let my head loll on my shoulders, Denny's fingers in my hair, touching my ears. I closed my eyes, my chest aching. If I just left it alone. Then Brad would be all right. If I forced anyone else to come forward then it would make everything worse. I felt myself falling backwards on to the bed, Denny tangled up with me, his kisses harder, his hands pushing at my jacket. I pulled myself up and struggled out of it, throwing it off the bed.

'Wait,' he said, his voice husky. 'Wait.'

I paused, hardly breathing, my mouth open.

'Here,' he said, pulling my hand towards him. 'Undress me . . . undress me . . .'

My fingers shaking, I undid the buttons of his shirt. I kissed his chest and he moaned, pushing himself back into the duvet.

'The rest,' he said, his voice cracking, pushing my hands lower.

I was light-headed. I was dizzy. Like being on a spinning roundabout and not wanting to come off. He lay back and I ran my hands across his skin. I could feel the tension in his limbs. I breathed deep and long and sank into the dark shadows on the bed.

Afterwards, as I watched him get dressed, I felt odd. I sat up and leaned my back on the headboard. I pulled at my clothes, straightening them. My legs were restless, my knees moving from side to side. Denny didn't seem to notice. He pulled on some jeans and a T-shirt. He threaded his belt through and zipped his jeans up. He glanced up and I caught his eye. He looked pleased with himself. I felt out of sorts, though, my skin hot, my clothes too tight. I wanted to take his hand and pull him back on to the bed. To get lost in the dark afternoon, to lie back and feel my own limbs tense.

The thought of it made me blush, fierce and hot. I lifted my legs off the bed and saw, on the floor, the two glasses of Coke that hadn't been touched. I picked one up and drank it down.

He sat down beside me.

'You all right?' he said, his voice sounding hushed in the quiet.

I nodded.

'Good girl. I've got a couple of things to do. Why don't you come along for the ride?'

I got up. A ride in the car with him. It cheered me up.

## 15

I got into Denny's car and he drove off.

'I've just got to pick something up.'

We'd only travelled a few minutes when he pulled over. We were on the edge of the Waterways estate. It was the second time I'd been there that day.

'Charlie, open that, will you?' he said, pointing. 'There's a key there? Pass it.'

I opened the glove compartment which was packed full. At the side was a key that had a skull key fob. It looked like a child's toy. I pulled it out and gave it to him.

'I use one of the lock-ups round here for some spare car parts. I just need to check something. I'll only be a minute . . .'

I watched as he disappeared down an alleyway at the side of a newsagent's. I opened the door and hung my legs out on the pavement. It was still hot. I fanned myself with my hands, watching people slouching by in the afternoon heat. It was after five. Not the best time to go home, especially if my mother was going to be there.

He appeared after a short while holding a bag. He got in the car and shoved it on the back seat. He leaned across and gave me a quick kiss on the side of my face.

'I'm going over to a mate's at Hawks Oak. Come with me if you want. Be a couple of hours?'

Hawks Oak. The words made me sit up. *Hawks Oak*. He started the car and drove away. As if he didn't need an answer.

'I've got a friend over there,' I said, quickly. 'You could drop me off. Abercrombie Road. It's opposite the new hospital.'

'OK,' he said, pleasantly.

For ten minutes I listened as he hummed to music. The closer we got the more apprehensive I felt. Maybe I should just go to his mate's after all, I thought. Then we stopped and the car was idling by a sign that said *Abercrombie Road*.

'Here we are!' he said, smiling at me.

I got out and watched until his car disappeared from view. Across the road was the new hospital. Not exactly *new* any more. I turned away. A heavy feeling took hold of me. Hawks Oak. A development of houses on land that had previously belonged to an industrial estate. I walked down Abercrombie Road, towards the small park that I remembered from years before. It held some swings and a small slide. When I got to it I opened the latched gate and went in and sat on the only bench. Underneath my feet the grass had turned to dry mud.

It was five-thirty and my mother would probably be in my house talking to my dad and possibly Brad if he had been allowed home by the police. I wondered where they would sit. In the living-room? Would my dad bring in a tray with some cups and saucers? Would my mum sit in my favourite chair? The one I used for my quiet time in the mornings?

Possibly they would stand in the kitchen. My dad might offer a drink but my mother would say, *No, I can't stay long. I've got to get back to Paul.* Paul Simon, my dad's younger brother, only a teenager when my mum and dad got married. I'd seen photographs of him, looking awkward in a suit and big shoes, his hair short and spiked up with gel. When he came back from university he wore it long. He was Uncle Paul and he played with me and Brad, and Mum, as it turned out.

I shivered. I looked around the play area at the swings which hung still. The slide had some letters painted along the side, an attempt at graffiti. It was odd to see, in such a pretty street, where all the houses were expensive and the gardens were well looked after. I wanted to look up, across the road to the house opposite, but I didn't let myself. I fiddled about with my jacket and then pulled my mobile out of my pocket. The message icon was there. I had two texts. One from my dad and one from Emily.

*Brad home on bail. Love Dad.*

*Come to IKEA tomorrow. It will take your mind off things XX*

Brad was home. That was a relief.

I reread Emily's message and felt mildly guilty. I hadn't told her everything. I'd kept important bits of the story to myself. I found myself staring at the house opposite. Number 34. It still looked the same as it had six years before. A pretty house in a quiet street where well-heeled people lived. A breeze came out of nowhere and made the swing shudder.

It was the same swing that I'd sat on all those years ago. My brother had sat on the other one. It was winter. A February day when the air was crisp and chunky with cold and the sky was the colour of the Mediterranean sea. We'd waited for hours. That's what it seemed like. Moving back and forth on the swings, not talking much, our eyes boring into the house across the road.

He'd been thirteen and I was ten. He'd come to my school at lunch-time. He'd told the teacher that he was taking me for a dental appointment. I was surprised. I didn't know anything about the appointment. I was only ten but I usually remembered things like that. We walked for a while and then I demanded to know what was happening.

'A dentist appointment?'

He was out of sorts, walking ahead of me, his shoulders rounded. When we got a few streets away from school he stopped suddenly.

'Want to see Mum?' he said.

I was thrown. Mum? What did he mean? Mum was in Australia, had been for years and years, as far back as I could remember. We were going to go and see her when we were old enough to fly on a plane by ourselves. I looked curiously at my thirteen-year-old brother.

Brad was tall and skinny at that age. His school uniform, as ever, was battered and askew. His tie shortened to a couple of inches, looking like a tongue poking out from his collar. His jacket was undone, showing a grubby shirt and dusty trousers. I sighed. Even though I tried to hang his clothes up for him they always looked as though they'd been lying in a heap all night. He had a rucksack over one shoulder that looked like it was holding bricks. On his feet were trainers, their laces loose. He wasn't allowed to wear them to school but somehow he always ended up in them.

We did a lot of stuff together, me and Brad. With Mum gone and Dad out at work for a lot of the time we looked after each other. After a long period of upset we settled into a comfortable way of living. Brad took me to school and anywhere else I needed to go. We went shopping together, to the supermarket, him pushing the trolley, me choosing the food. We went swimming, to the park, out on bikes. I was his little sister and until the age of about eight or nine I had to be looked after by him at all times.

I did my bit. When Dad was around I helped him with the housework and cooking. When Dad was out I did what I could myself. I could make beans on toast from the age of six and by the time I was nine or ten could do a whole meal. I liked it. In the kitchen I was in charge.

Brad and me were like a miniature married couple. We rubbed along together. We didn't talk about Mum. She was a face in some photographs that we rarely looked at. She was a sore spot that neither of us prodded. I didn't know what Brad thought about her. I knew that when I did think of her I pictured her standing next to a kangaroo. Her face was vague but her long hair was blowing in the breeze and hanging across her chest was the guitar. She was far away, untouchable. I didn't have strong feelings about her, just memories and a notion that one day I would see her again.

I had no idea that it would be on a February afternoon on the other side of town.

'Do you want to see Mum?' Brad repeated.

'In Australia?' I said.

'We have to get a bus. Come on,' he said, not answering.

We had to get two buses and it took over an hour. On the journey Brad tried to explain. His words tumbled out. He said them angrily. He pulled at his tie and played with the zipper on his jacket. He swore and I looked round the bus hoping that no one was listening. Because it was lunch-time we didn't look out of place. Our bus passed knots of schoolchildren on the pavement, in front of chip shops, hanging around sweet shops and burger vans. We got off at the town centre and then found the second bus. Then it was quieter, not so many kids around.

It was the second time that day that Brad had done the journey. He'd been in the town centre earlier and seen her. At first he'd hardly been able to believe his eyes. He'd been with a couple of his mates on his way to school and after a moment or two he'd left them and walked off after her. Once or twice he'd stopped and decided to leave it, to go back the way he came.

He hadn't though.

She had a pushchair and had taken her time to get on and off the bus. She'd been flustered, Brad said, and hadn't noticed him. In any case it was six years since she'd seen him. He'd changed. We'd both changed. Our mother had changed. He'd gone to the back of the bus and sat behind a magazine and waited for her to pull her bags and her baby together and drag her folded-up pushchair off the bus. He followed her from a distance and saw her go into number 34 Abercrombie Road.

It wasn't a long walk from the bus stop but I'd dragged behind my brother, my feet and legs tired. When we got to the park Brad dumped his bag and sat on the swing. I followed suit but placed my bag neatly on the edge of the bench.

'I don't get it,' I said. 'Why does Mum live here? I thought she lived in Australia.'

Brad didn't say much. All the while that we were swinging there I looked at the house and remembered things about it. The door was bright red, like a postbox. The windows were dark wood and there were no net curtains on them. Upstairs the curtain were shut. I wondered if my mum was in that room, maybe with her baby, having an afternoon nap.

Suddenly Brad jumped off the swing and walked out of the park and across the street. It took me a moment to follow, picking up my bag and then pulling his along. I struggled after him and then we were standing at the glossy front door that had two bubbly glass panels in it. Brad's finger was on the bell and I could hear it ringing on and on and I looked around the street with embarrassment, afraid that other people might come out of their houses. When I looked back I saw a shape through the glass. It was indistinct, coming from far away and getting bigger, like someone surfacing from deep water. The door opened and there she was.

'Yes?' she said testily.

She had a baby on her hip. He was big, maybe six or nine months old. He was wearing little blue jeans and a jumper and velvet slippers tied at the ankle. He had his fist in his mouth and his eyes looked huge and he focused on me and Brad, like two waifs washed up at his mum's door.

'What?' she said and then in a second she seemed to stagger back a step and recognition was written all over her face. 'Oh my God!'

Brad turned and walked away. I stood for a second staring at her.

'Wait!' she said, moving forward as though she was going to run after him but then looking down at the baby on her hip.

'Brad,' she called, and then looking at me, she said, 'Charlotte! Oh Charlotte!'

'You've had your hair cut!' I said.

And she had. Gone were the baby waves and the long silk strands. Instead it was short and spiky and bits of it were sticking bolt upright on top of her head. It looked horrible. I turned, carrying Brad's bag and my own, and strode off after him. I could hear her follow for a few steps but I didn't look around. I just remembered her flowing tresses, splayed across her shoulders. Hair that smelled of lemon and tickled my skin. *I would never have it cut*, she'd said.

A lie.

It was after six now. I was tired of visiting the past. I

walked back to the main road and jumped on a bus. I sat at the back and remembered that day, all those years before, when me and Brad went home and told Dad.

'Your mother's here? In England? Where?' he'd said.

'Hawks Oak? That new estate? The one off the ring road?' he said, later. 'I don't believe it,' he said. 'I knew they'd come back from Australia but . . .'

'And they're living here, in this town?'

'She's got a *baby*?'

My dad had made a cup of tea which he didn't drink. He'd got out the lawnmower but didn't cut the grass. He'd put the television on but sat looking out of the window. It wasn't long before my mum had arrived at the front door. Brad and me ran upstairs to his room. We sat on the floor with our backs against the door as we had when they were splitting up. This time things were different. We sat apart, our shoulders set, our arms rigid. His trainers looked huge beside my leather shoes. His head hung on to his chest.

We could hear the voices. Not angry this time, just a continual murmur. After a while Brad stood up and so did I. He went out of the room and I watched as he walked downstairs and went into the living-room. The door shut and I could hear the sound of his voice alongside those of Dad and Mum. I went downstairs and opened the front door intending to go out, to walk around until they'd gone. But a car was outside. My uncle Paul was in the front seat, his shoulders rounded, his fingers tapping impatiently on the steering wheel. In the back I could see the baby seat and the baby's profile. A new baby. A boy. Maybe our mum would have another, a little girl, and then she would have a replacement family.

She had been living in Abercrombie Road for three months and intended to contact us, she said, just as soon as they'd become settled. Of course she intended to contact us. We were her children, she loved us. She wanted us to visit, to stay overnight, to have tea, to get to know the new baby.

We never did. We didn't want to see her.

Six years later I still didn't want to see her. I changed buses at the city centre and sat watching as the streets and houses and shops sped by. I felt the roads stretching out behind me; the distance between Abercrombie Road and our house. It was a continent away.

My dad's face had lifted when we told him that we didn't want anything to do with her. He was relieved. He painted the outside of the house in the days that followed, changing the colours, buying a new front door. It was as if we'd moved and started all over again. Only this time we'd left our mother behind instead of the other way around.

# 16

My dad was in the kitchen when I got home. He was reading some papers and leaflets that were spread across the table. I glanced down and saw a few key words: *Legal Aid, Your Solicitor, Crown Court: What You Need to Know.*

'It's going to be all right,' he said.

'All right?'

I sat down opposite him. He used the sides of his hands to straighten up the papers. I inhaled and sensed an unusual smell. A flowery perfume. My mother had been in here, perhaps sitting in this same chair. From above there was the distant sound of music coming from Brad's room.

'We've got a good solicitor. He says the police won't be able to prove Manslaughter. The most they'll get is Criminal Damage.'

I thought of Denny. They were almost his words. It should have calmed me but strangely it didn't.

'It'll work out,' my dad said, sorting through the papers in front of him. An orange Post-it stood out. I read the upside-down words: *From Max Robbins.*

'But someone died,' I said.

I stared at my dad, willing him to say something

reassuring. He shrugged his shoulders as if to say, *I don't know.*

'It could have been you, driving to work. You sometimes use the M25.'

'It's a tragedy, Charlie. But that doesn't mean Brad should take the blame. He says he didn't do it. Remember?'

'I thought you didn't believe him?'

'I didn't say that . . . Anyway I've got to stand by him. He's my son.'

I nodded. There didn't seem to be much more to say. My dad opened his mouth but then seemed to think better of it. Perhaps he was going to talk about my mother. I didn't want to hear what she thought about it so I went upstairs.

I had a shower. I wanted to wash the day away. I got a towel and went into the bathroom, ignoring my brother's door and the music that was throbbing away. I stood in the water for ages, letting it bore into my back. Then I dried myself and stood naked in front of the bathroom mirror.

I had a long white body. A boy's body. My tiny breasts looked flat and my ribs stood out. My legs were stringy and my stomach concave. I looked like I needed a good meal. I remembered Denny's body from earlier. He was chunky and solid. His thighs had muscles and his hips and back looked strong. His chest and legs were dark with fluffy hairs. He had a man's body. What would he think of mine? I tried to look at myself from his point of view. I pushed my breasts together to make a cleavage line. I stood with one leg in front of the other as if posing for a photograph. Then I stopped and looked at my reflection with impatience. When was I going to look like a woman?

Would Denny want me more then?

Denny had been right about Brad. *He's a man now. Let him make his own decisions.* How stupid I must have looked. Rushing in, asking him to own up. Racing round to Billy Warner's house as though I was some kind of private detective. Denny must have laughed at me. And yet he hadn't been laughing that afternoon, on his bed, my fingers stroking the hairs on his thigh.

The front door bell rang and it startled me. I pulled my towel tightly around my chest. My dad's voice sounded and I heard Denny. A feeling of exhilaration went through me. It was unexpected. To see him again so soon! I opened the door a crack but shut it quickly as Denny came running up the stairs calling to Brad. I backed up to the bath and sat on the edge.

Maybe he would stay a while. Maybe Brad and Dad would go to bed and leave the two of us alone. I found myself breathing lightly, my mouth going dry. But then I heard him say goodbye. I crept over to the door and opened it slightly.

'Just hang in there,' Denny said, out in the hallway. 'It'll all be over soon.'

His words were soothing. I closed my eyes for a moment and thought of him whispering to me.

'I don't know if I can. Today, I almost . . .'

My brother's voice was cracking. Denny stepped back and into his room.

'You didn't say anything about me?' he hissed, his words low and husky.

'No, no. But it was on the tip of my tongue. I wanted to say, *We did it! We did it. We didn't mean to but we did it!*'

Denny disappeared into Brad's room and I stood frozen to the spot. I pulled the towel tightly round me so that I could hardly breathe. I moved out of the bathroom and along the hall and stood close to my brother's door. I heard their voices, my brother's halting, cracking; Denny's was firm but unsure.

'They were talking about it at the station. I heard them. They were talking about the body. It was awful, Den. Awful. I started to think that maybe it would be better if we . . . If we owned up. We didn't mean it.'

'Don't you say a word about me, Brad. If you're gonna confess you do it yourself. Don't pull me in . . .'

'I just thought . . .'

'Don't think . . . What difference is it gonna make now? What's done is done!'

*What's done is done.* A line from Macbeth. An essay I did about the effect of murder on Macbeth's wife. *What's done is done*, she'd cried.

Denny's voice became louder. He was coming out.

'Brad, you don't grass, right?'

As I was retreating to the bathroom I heard my brother murmur something. I closed the door behind me and stood rigid. Denny's footsteps receded down the stairs. Then I sat down on the floor leaning against the door. Denny had lied to me. He had been there on that footbridge with Brad.

Was it Denny who threw the stone?

# Thursday

# 17

The footbridge was crowded. Tony Haskins found himself shuffling to the side to make room for a man with a camera. Next to him was Dom Kennedy, looking downwards in a respectful way, as if he was in church. Underneath, the traffic sped past, oblivious to what was happening above. Fifteen or so people milling about a bridge that spanned the busy motorway.

'This is the second of these I've been to in as many days,' Dom said, his voice a loud whisper.

Tony nodded, straining to hear Dom's words above the traffic. He was talking about the accident on the high street. A silver car hitting a girl who was standing at a bus stop. One little girl dead, her friend in shock. A hit-and-run driver. Probably someone who was drunk. That was usually the reason.

'It was bigger than this,' Dom said. 'Fifty or more people there, I'd say. And the television people.'

'A dead child is more newsworthy than a dead lorry driver,' Tony said. 'This'll just about make the local paper.'

A hush went over the crowd. A woman and a teenager

were leading some people walking down the lane from the forest side of the motorway. The woman was holding a wreath and the girl a bunch of flowers. Paul Sullivan's wife and daughter. Mrs Sullivan was wearing trousers and a loose blouse, her daughter had on jeans and a T-shirt. He'd expected them to be in black but they were dressed in ordinary everyday clothes. The girl was linking her mother's arm and seemed shy at the number of people who were waiting for them. Tony glanced sideways at Dom and caught his eye, exchanging knowing looks. The parents, the wives, the husbands, the children; they all looked as though they'd lost their way in a strange land. Tony smoothed his tie down and pinched at the creases in his trousers.

A strident car horn sounded from down below. Tony turned and looked over the rail. Headlights were flashing with irritation as one car swept in front of another. Was it the car that had hooted? Probably not. At the speed these cars were going it was most likely a mile or two up the road by the time he looked. What was it – seventy? Or eighty? Or maybe even ninety miles an hour? All it took was a moment's loss of concentration or a bad judgement or even a stone flung from a footbridge which shattered a windscreen. Then one tried to stop, then the next and the next and one by one they slammed into each other in some horrible dance. Usually there were fires as petrol tanks exploded. At least in this crash that hadn't happened.

A man was still dead though. A husband, a father. Someone like himself.

Mrs Sullivan and her daughter walked to the middle of the bridge. Tony noticed a couple of other people who seemed to be with them, relatives or friends perhaps. The man with a camera began taking photographs. Mrs Sullivan bent over and placed the wreath in an upright position, leaning against the wire. The girl lay the flowers on the base of the footbridge. They stood up and there was a moment's silence. Tony Haskins wondered if someone was going to say something. A man started to talk, a relative, perhaps. Tony leaned against the rail. He couldn't really hear what was being said so he looked down at the traffic.

He wondered if this was the very spot where Brad had stood when he threw the stone. But was it Brad who had done it? Or had he been cavorting around on the footbridge while some other idiot threw it?

Stupid, brainless, hopeless Bradley.

How many times had Tony come into contact with the lad over the last few years? Too many to count. Wherever there was petty crime he seemed to pop up. No doubt he saw himself an apprentice hard man. He would spend his youth gathering the scars of this and that court sentence. He would bear them with some sort of pride, thinking that it made him important in his own little world. Then he'd do something big; an armed robbery or some aggravated burglary. He'd hurt someone or even kill them. He'd end up with a life sentence.

Tony Haskins looked over at the grieving mother and daughter, leaning on each other, both in tears. If Brad could see the effects of this. If he could meet this woman and her daughter. Maybe it would change him. Maybe it would put the brakes on this drift into criminality.

'The little girl who got killed?' Dom whispered.

Tony Haskins turned to face him.

'The car mounted the pavement and hit her at speed. She never stood a chance. Nine years old. Pretty as a picture. Wanted to be a dancer when she grew up.'

There was a mumble of conversation and Tony Haskins watched as the woman and the girl walked away back up the forest track, followed by their friends.

'A ballerina,' Dom said.

Tony Haskins nodded. What could he say? What could anyone say?

# 18

I saw Billy Warner through the car window, strolling along as though he didn't have a care in the world. For once he wasn't in a car and looked quite smart, as though he had a job interview to go to.

It was lunch-time and we were on our way back from IKEA. Emily's mum was driving, Emily in the passenger seat. I was in the back. Beside me were several bags full of stuff for the newly decorated bedroom. Emily's mum was talking and Emily was answering, every now and then saying, *That's right, isn't it, Charlie?* Or *What do you think, Charlie?* When we stopped at the traffic lights Mrs Little turned round and asked me if I was OK, if I had enough space beside all the purchases, if I was feeling a bit better about everything. They were both looking after me.

I gave a bright smile and turned back to the window but I was feeling weary and flat. I hadn't intended to go to IKEA but the only other choice was to stay at home and shuffle round the house trying to avoid my brother and my dad. More than anything I wanted to keep myself busy in case I was tempted to go and see Denny.

Billy Warner came into my sight when we swung into the one-way system round the town centre. We got into some slow-moving traffic and I watched him walking into the entrance of the mall. It took me a few moments to place him, to remember why it was that I wanted to see him. I made a snap decision. I clicked open my seat belt and when the car came to a complete stop I butted into the conversation.

'I've got to go. I just remembered something I have to do. I'll ring you later, Emily. Thanks for taking me, Mrs Little.'

Before anyone could turn round to look at me or ask any questions I had the back door open and I was out striding across the road towards the shopping mall. I didn't even glance back. The warm air hung about me and I skipped the last couple of paces until I was in the revolving doors of the mall and felt the cold air-conditioning on my face.

Once inside I looked round. Some way ahead, just walking past a group of security men, was Billy Warner. I quickened up and went after him. The mall was busy and I had to sidestep several people. A couple of mums with pushchairs blocked my way and I had to wait while they moved off into a shop.

'Billy!' I called but he didn't hear.

I got past the central display stand and looked around. I couldn't see him anywhere. I peered into a couple of shops but he wasn't there. I stood very still, my eyes looking as far up the mall as I could. Then I saw him. He wasn't shopping after all, he was heading for the far exit. I followed.

'Billy,' I shouted.

He was walking across the gardens that led to the Town

Hall. He must have heard something because he turned and looked back. Maybe he actually saw me. Whatever. He picked up speed and I had to almost run to catch up with him. He went round the corner and when I followed I saw him walking towards his mum who was waiting outside the magistrates' court. She was dressed in a dark suit as if she was going to a funeral. She held a cigarette in the air. When he got to her she rummaged in her bag and offered him one. He shook his head.

I huffed. I didn't want to say a word to him if Mrs Warner was there. I stood at the corner of the building for a few moments feeling a bit silly, then I turned and walked off. Billy Warner up in front of the magistrate again. That was no surprise.

I went back towards the mall. It was easier to cut through the air-conditioned shopping centre than to walk the long way round to the bus stop.

That's when I saw Denny. He was coming down the escalators. It surprised me and I moved forward for a second, my instinct to go towards him. Then I saw Tania Nicholls leaning in towards him, linking his arm in a proprietorial way.

Of course. It was his lunch-hour and his office was nearby. I backed away and stood in a shop doorway. I remembered his words the night before. *Don't say a word about me, Brad . . . Don't pull me in.* After all the things he had said to me. *On my mother's life I wasn't on that footbridge.* A lie. A Big Lie.

Tania Nicholls had done something to her hair. Pulled it

up on top of her head. It made her look taller and a little more sophisticated. She had huge hoop earrings on and her shoulders were bare, just two shoelace straps holding up a tight dress that hugged her body, making her breasts stick out. I folded my arms across my chest in consternation.

What was he doing with her? Why were they together? Hadn't they rowed a couple of evenings before? Hadn't he spent time with me? Private time. The two of us in his bedroom. Didn't that mean something?

All thoughts of my brother dropped out of my head and I watched with dismay as the two of them walked on. Denny leaned down and said something into Tania's ear. Her face broke into a scandalized smile. What was it he said? I wondered. *Touch me, Kiss me, Bite me. The way I taught you. Do it, Do it.*

I felt a blush creep up my neck. I tried to cover it with my hands. I kept my eye on the couple as they sauntered along, looking happy, contented, satisfied. In love.

I knew then that I should have stayed in the car with Emily and her mum.

# 19

I went home. I walked into the kitchen and found Brad making himself a cup of tea. He offered me one and I sat down. He was looking a bit wild. His hair was sticking up and he had an unironed shirt on over some shorts. It was done up on the wrong button and I wanted to reach across and fix it. He shuffled around, taking a mug from the drainer and putting the tea bag in it without drying it first. Then he overfilled it with boiling water and it spilled over the side. He grumbled quietly and got a tea towel and cleared up.

I felt my irritation build up as I watched him. How had he become so hopeless? When we were younger, when our mother left, he'd held everything together. Now he couldn't make a cup of tea without messing up. When he pushed the mug across the table I mumbled a thanks and let it sit gently steaming between us.

'Where you been?' he said.

'Out with Emily,' I answered.

There was no expression on his face. It was as if he hadn't even heard my answer or didn't care if he had. He was probably too preoccupied with his own problems. Despite what Dad said it was a pity I couldn't be more like

Brad. Then I wouldn't be so anxious, so wound up. I could just say, *Brad's a man, let him sort his own life out.* But he was my brother and I felt this burst of sympathy for him. In any case the sullen youth in front of me was so different to the voice I had heard the previous evening. *We did it! We did it! We didn't mean to but we did!* He'd sounded like an eleven-year-old. A boy who'd thrown a stone and broken a window. *Let's own up, let's give some pocket money so that it can be fixed.* Only this time the window was in a moving lorry and nothing could be fixed. Brad wanted to own up but Denny wouldn't let him. Denny wouldn't help him. Brad needed me and Dad. He needed *me*.

'Have you spoken to your solicitor today?' I said.

He shrugged as if to say, *What's the point?*

'Someone's dead, Brad,' I said. 'Don't you care? Don't you have any feelings about it?'

'Course I do,' he said, sulkily.

Did he care? It was hard to tell. I stood up and took my mug to the sink and poured the tea away. I let the tap run until the sink was clean. Then I picked up the spent tea bag from the drainer and let it drop into the pedal bin. Maybe I should just leave it. Let him sort his own mess out.

'I do care, Charlie.'

I looked round at him. His face had reddened and his eyes were glassy. I opened my mouth to speak but my words deserted me.

'I never meant anyone to get hurt. It was just a laugh,' he said, and hiccupped as though he was going to burst into tears.

'Oh, Brad,' I said, putting my hands on his shoulders. 'Maybe if you just made a confession. Told the whole story to the police. That way you could get it off your chest. Let them see the whole picture. At the moment everyone is blaming you. But it wasn't just you.'

He shook me off.

'I'm saying nothing to the police.'

'It'll make you feel better if you talk to someone,' I said, walking back to my chair and sitting down.

'I talked to Mum,' he said.

I frowned. I didn't want to hear anything about Mum.

'She's gonna help out. She's offered some money, you know for legal bills.'

I didn't say a word.

'Thing is . . . I saw her a while back. She brought her car into the garage for a service.'

A while back. Before any of this happened.

'She said it was a coincidence, that I was the last person she expected to see. I'm not sure though. I think she might have made a point of finding me.'

I felt my face hardening.

'Mum would like to see you. She'd like to talk to you.'

'But we agreed. We didn't want to see her. We *agreed*.'

'That was a long time ago,' he said, looking more composed. 'She's not like I remember. She's different. She's nice.'

I stared over at him. *Nice! Nice!* She left us to go and live in Australia. Then she came back and hid for a while on the other side of the town centre. She replaced us with a brand new baby. I wanted to say all these things but they hung in the air between us. Once me and Brad had sat together with our backs against the door listening to her go. Now we were sitting facing each other, a table holding us apart. I got up. I didn't want to hear any more of what he had to say. I walked out of the room just as the front door key sounded and the door opened.

My dad stood there looking sheepish. Behind him was my mother.

'Here's Charlie,' he said, lightly.

His lips were bunched up though as if to say, *Charlie, I had no choice but to bring her*.

'Hello, Charlotte,' she said.

She looked different to when I last saw her. She'd put on weight. Her hair was no longer spiky and short. It curled around her ears and had been coloured a shade of red. She was wearing lipstick and brightly coloured earrings that matched her top. She looked nothing like the mother I remembered.

'Your mum's here to see Brad.'

No she wasn't. She was here to see me. She could see Brad any time at the garage where she'd found him. She could speak to him on the phone. He was available for her. No, she'd come to see me.

'He's in there.'

I gestured to the kitchen. Then I picked up my mobile and keys. I walked up to my dad and gave him a kiss on the cheek. Without a word I brushed past my mother and went out of the house.

## 20

Emily's bedroom looked like one of the model rooms in IKEA. It was compact yet there was lots of space. It was full of shelves, boxes, containers. There were special hooks for things and pinboards as well as a magnetic notice-board.

'It's nice,' I said, nodding my head.

'Nice?' she said, her arms folded. 'Is that the best you can come up with?'

'Well, no. It's brilliant.'

Emily was annoyed at me. I walked over to her bed and sat on the edge.

'These colours are very restful,' I said.

She seemed to tighten the fold in her arms. Then she gave an exaggerated sigh and sat cross-legged on the new IKEA rug, midnight blue with pink and grey overlapping squares.

'I know you're going through a lot at the moment but you can't just shut me out!'

*Shut me out.* It wasn't the sort of phrase Emily used.

'I feel like you're excluding me. We've been friends for years but you didn't even tell me about your mum. And then you just leap out of my mum's car and run off. It made me look like an idiot!'

She was playing with the ends of her hair, twisting it round her finger. She looked uncomfortable. I felt bad for her. She'd always been the dominant one, in charge of me, sure that I'd go along with whatever she wanted to do.

'I'm sorry . . . You know, with Brad and everything . . .'

She shuffled towards me. 'I do know. I'm really sorry about your brother. I can help, I'm sure I can. But it's like you're not really telling me everything.'

She was right. I should open up to her. I should let her know what was going on in my life. Not just about Brad but about my mother as well. Then there was Denny to think about. Poor Emily. She thought she knew me, knew every facet of my personality.

'I think Denny was on the footbridge with Brad,' I said unsteadily. 'I heard him and Brad talking last night. Denny was telling Brad to keep him out of it. He virtually admitted he was there.'

'Dennis Scott?' Emily said, wrinkling up her nose. 'That doesn't surprise me.'

'What do you mean?' I said.

'Don't you remember when he and your brother were at school? Dennis Scott always looked like the swot. He was always well dressed and his books in his bag. I don't remember him being on report or in any trouble or suspended.'

I nodded.

'But everyone said he was selling cannabis. And there was a rumour about him. A girl in our year? Susan somebody, Reeves, I think. She was his cousin. She left school in year eight? To have a baby? Everyone said it was his.'

'I don't remember any of this.'

'Maybe it was before we were in the same form. Anyhow you were always too wound up with what was happening to Brad.'

I moved round, feeling uncomfortable. I was learning things I'd rather not know.

'I don't know what to do about any of this. I just don't want my brother to take the blame by himself.'

'If we could just find Billy Warner . . .'

'Oh!' I said. 'I saw him this morning. That's why I jumped out of your mum's car. He went into the magistrates' court before I could speak to him.'

Emily looked at her watch.

'We could talk to him. It's only three-thirty. He might still be there. We should go. Mum'll give us a lift!'

She'd jumped up and grabbed her bag off her desk. She was fired up, in charge again.

'Come on. At least we'll be doing something,' she said, as if seeing Billy Warner would sort everything out.

Why not? I thought. It wasn't as if I had anything else to do.


Her mum dropped us off at the town centre and we walked through the mall towards the Town Hall and civic buildings. I led the way. I'd been there before with Dad and Brad.

Past the Town Hall the magistrates' court was set back

off the pavement, surrounded by pretty gardens and benches. Outside were small knots of people in huddles sucking on cigarettes or just involved in intense conversations. Just like Mrs Warner and Billy had been. Emily was walking briskly as though she had an appointment to get to; I was hanging behind, not really sure if I wanted to know the truth once and for all. Didn't I know enough? That Denny was with Brad even though he'd said he wasn't. *On my mother's life*, he'd whispered. I thought of my own mother pushing herself into Brad's life, helping out with money. Maybe she was the one who would help Brad now, not me. Seeing Billy Warner was just something to do; to keep me busy while everything else was spiralling out of my control.

We walked into the main foyer. Emily stopped and looked around, her eye settling on an impressive floor-to-ceiling notice-board. I took her arm. I knew the way. We went through some revolving doors and followed the arrow to the public area. It was a long wide corridor with benches and drinks machines and No Smoking signs every few yards. In the corner, perched up high, was a television set showing cartoons. I'd watched it in the past. There were four sets of double doors which I knew were the entrances to the courts.

It was four o'clock and pretty quiet, just a few tired-looking people sitting on the seats, some drinking from plastic cups, others just staring into space. The two nearest doors creaked open and a man in a suit came out, carrying a briefcase and folders under his arm. He was followed by a couple of others and a woman in a white dress that was creased across the middle.

'Where do you think he'll be?' Emily said, her eyes darting around, taking it all in.

I didn't answer. I walked ahead of her down the length of the corridor pausing at each of the doors, hearing strong voices and general mumblings. At one door there was complete silence, their business for the day having ended, I assumed.

'I don't know,' I said when I got back to Emily. 'Maybe if we just sit down for a while and see if he appears . . .'

We sat on a bench. We were only there for a few minutes when I saw Mrs Warner bursting out of the doors near the far end. She was walking rapidly, her heels tapping along the floor. She looked quite respectable in her dark clothes. I wondered if her nails were still chequered.

Behind her were a couple of people and then Billy, walking at a leisurely pace, his hands in the pockets of his suit. He had a pleasant expression on his face as if he'd just come out of a cinema. I wondered what he'd done.

'Quick,' I said, standing up.

Emily and I stood to the side as Mrs Warner shot past us without any sign of recognition and headed for the women's toilets. Just before she went in she paused, looking round at her son.

'Wait there!' she commanded.

We stood still, watching Billy Warner's shoulders slump. He saw us and looked puzzled. He sat heavily on one of the benches, his legs splayed out so that a couple of people had to step out of the way to avoid tripping over his feet.

'What's up?' he said when Emily and I sat down on either side of him.

'What did you do?' Emily said.

'Nothing,' he replied sulkily.

'Don't tell me they found you not guilty? That's a laugh!'

'It weren't me. It was my mum. She's had some trouble with a neighbour and she was up for Criminal Damage.'

Emily was thrown for a moment. Then she continued speaking.

'OK, then, we believe you. But we know you were there on the M25 footbridge, last Sunday when that bad accident happened. Dennis Scott told us.'

My mouth opened. Why did she say that? Billy looked surprised.

'Denny grassed me up?' he said.

'Not exactly,' I mumbled.

'It's only a matter of time before the police find out,' Emily said, with authority. 'You should own up before they come and arrest you.'

'Get lost,' he said, standing up, shaking each leg in turn, as if he'd been sitting down for hours.

The door of the Ladies opened and his mum came out. She had applied bright red lipstick and was shaking her hands as if they weren't quite dry. She was scowling.

'I don't suppose your mum would be very pleased that you threw that stone,' Emily said. 'Causing a massive accident. Maybe we'll tell her! What do you think, Charlie?'

Billy Warner turned to me. His cheeks were red with sudden annoyance.

'Dennis Scott never told you I was on that bridge, Charlic, and neither did your brother. They would never grass anybody up.'

'Billy!' Mrs Warner shouted across the public area.

'I don't know why you're poking your nose in this. Leave your brother's business alone.'

'Someone died!' Emily hissed.

'Nobody meant that to happen,' Billy said, under his breath.

'Brad never threw that stone and he's being charged with Manslaughter!' I said.

'Anyway,' Emily cut across me, 'maybe Brad will inform on you. Maybe when it comes to the trial and two or three years in prison he won't want to take the blame himself.'

'I don't know what your brother will do! I haven't got a clue! But he won't be able to say who was on that footbridge. Neither him nor Dennis Scott. Because they weren't there last Sunday. Neither of them. Got it? I don't know where they were but they weren't on that footbridge when that accident happened. So neither of them can grass on anyone!'

Mrs Warner started to walk in our direction and Billy shoved his way past me and met her halfway. Emily and I watched speechless as they disappeared out of the revolving doors.

'What did he just say?' Emily said.

Billy Warner's words were ringing inside my head.

'He said that Brad wasn't on the footbridge when the accident happened. Neither was Denny.'

We sat down on a bench. Neither of us spoke.

*On my mother's life. I wasn't there.* Denny had said it and he had told the truth.

'So how come your brother said he was there?' Emily said. 'That's the bit I don't understand!'

I didn't understand it either.

# Friday

# 21

Danielle woke up early. She lay still for a while listening to the noises outside. The dog was barking from a couple of gardens away. An angry yap and then a withering cry. A silence and then a few indignant barks. The owners left it out all night and all day, she knew that. It was something that had annoyed her dad, especially when he'd got back from a long drive and needed to catch up on his sleep.

'Why have a flaming dog,' he'd said, 'and dump it out in the garden?'

Danielle got up and pulled her cotton dressing-gown on. Not that she really needed it. It was going to be another hot day, she could tell. She went out into the hallway and stood at her mum's bedroom door. Her mum was fast asleep, her face calm and rested, her lips slightly open. She had her hand under her head. Danielle tutted. She would wake up with pins and needles. It happened to her often enough.

In the bathroom she rinsed her mouth and looked in the mirror. Her braces shone back at her. She sighed. Even after all these months they were still like horrible metal bars in front of her teeth. She had wanted them but they were a trial to wear. *Hey, Jaws, give us a smile*, her dad used to say. She always punched or nipped him when he said it but he just chortled with laughter. She ran her tongue along them and wondered how long it would be before they came off.

In the kitchen she made herself a cup of tea. She carried it out of the back door into the garden and heard the dog barking. Outside it sounded sad and lonely. *I've a good mind to go to the RSPCA*, her dad had said, but he never had.

She went into the garage. Her dad's huge CD collection was all along one wall. He'd built the shelving after Mum had refused to have them cluttering up the house any more. It was like a library. Alphabetically organized with small red cards placed where CDs had been removed for playing, either in the house, in Mum's car or in Dad's lorry. If he was on a long trip he sometimes took twenty or more with him. He'd theme it, she knew. The 1980s, Soul or Reggae or even Ballads by Sinatra and Bennett; singers that Danielle had never even heard of.

He loved those CDs.

Danielle sat on the plastic stool and felt her lips trembling. How could it be that she would never see him again? Dad with his big tummy and his calloused fingers? Putting on his hair gel in front of the bathroom, taking ages to get it right. *Not bad for an old bloke*, he'd say, winking at her and pretending to do some kind of silly disco dance.

A couple of the shelves at the bottom were empty where Mum had started to move the CDs back into the house. She hadn't wanted them there when Dad was alive but now that he was dead she'd decided that they should be in different rooms. Scattered around the house so that they could be seen and used more often. She'd offered Danielle the modern ones for her room. The rest would be stored in new cupboards that they were going to buy.

Danielle put her tea down and pulled out a CD. *Saturday Night Fever*. She knew this one. Her dad had played it at his last birthday party. He and Mum got in the middle of the front room and danced the same steps like John Travolta did in the film. She'd been so embarrassed. Her dad had tried to get her to do the steps but she'd stormed off upstairs in a mood. She'd sat at her dressing-table mirror and looked at her braces for ages.

She went outside, into the garden. She could hear it again. The lonely dog. A long sad yodel that seemed to pierce the morning silence. *Flaming dog!* her dad had said.

How she wished she could hear him say it now.

# 22

I watched out of the front bedroom window as my mother pulled up in her car. She took a moment to park, going back and forth a couple of times. I stood back from the glass as she got out, brushed her clothes down and walked up to our front door. The bell rang tentatively as if she didn't want to make too much noise. From downstairs I heard Dad's footsteps along the hallway and then the door opened.

I listened for a moment to the three voices overlapping. *Ready? Yes. Got everything? What time we due? Thanks for coming. Come on, Brad, let's get going. You look nice in that suit. So grown up! What time are we meeting the solicitor?*

'Bye, Charlie,' my dad called.

I didn't answer. There was a murmur of voices and then the front door shut. I crept back to the window and watched as the three of them got into my mum's car. Not one of them looked back. Not one of them. I walked along the landing to my own room and shut the door. I sat on the bed and crossed my arms. Everything was happening without me. I felt confused, frustrated, excluded.

I'd spoken to Brad the night before, as soon as I'd got back from the magistrates' court. I'd waltzed straight into his room, something I never do. He had been ironing his suit trousers. On the picture rail was a shirt on a hanger and hanging over one shoulder was a plain blue tie. Court clothes. I remembered from the last time. Glancing down I saw his shoes, polished and waiting to be worn.

'Yes?' he said, not at all friendly.

I hesitated. Billy Warner's news had thrown me. If Brad hadn't been there why had he said he was?

'I saw Billy Warner,' I said, walking across and sitting on his bed.

'So?'

'He said . . .'

'You don't want to believe a word he says.'

'He said you weren't there when the accident happened.'

'Did he? How does he know?'

'He was there.'

'Is that what he said?'

'Not exactly. He didn't exactly say *I was there* but the things he said suggest that.'

'You sound like the law. Actually, when I come to think about it, you'd make a good copper. *Little Miss Goody Two Shoes.*'

'Why are you being so horrible?' I said, gripping on to his duvet.

He stood erect, holding the bottoms of his suit trousers so that they hung upside down. Then he reached for a hanger and slid them on, making sure that the creases were flat.

'I just want you to keep out of it. Denny says you're on at him all the time. Now Billy Warner. Can't you just leave it alone?'

'Denny said that?'

A single arrow of hurt pricked me. Denny had been talking about me to Brad. Moaning about me. *Your little sister*, he might have said, *she's getting on my nerves, going on and on.* I bowed my head with shame.

My feelings about Denny were all mixed up. Before all this happened I knew what to expect when I thought about him. A warm feeling, an ache, a need to close my eyes and sink into the dark with him. It wasn't love, I knew that now. I knew he had a girlfriend. Now I just felt agitated, unhappy, as though there was this other Denny emerging, a stranger, someone I absolutely didn't know. First he was letting my brother take the blame, now the mystery was deeper. He was happy for me to undress him and yet he was complaining about me to Brad. I was just an interfering little sister. Maybe in his head he disapproved of other things. Charlie with her plain face and her boy's breasts. Poor Charlie. Brad's little sister. More like a boy than a girl. It was a muddle and I couldn't see a straight line through it.

Brad was sitting beside me. I'd been so tangled up in my own thoughts that I hadn't noticed.

'You can't believe what Billy said,' he said softly.

'But why would he lie? I could understand if he said you *were there* and he wasn't but what possible reason would he have for saying that?'

'He's an idiot!'

Brad's voice was dismissive but there was a tremble in his words.

'Why are you owning up to something you never did?'

'I didn't own up. The police came for me, remember.'

They had come for him. On Monday morning. A lifetime ago.

'That's right. And you were adamant that you weren't there. Why did you change your story?'

He stood up and walked across to the ironing-board. He picked up the iron and wound the flex around it. Then he reached underneath and let the catch go and the board folded in on itself. He leaned it against the wall.

'I never planned any of this, Charlie. None of it, right? It just sort of happened and you're going to have to trust me. What I'm doing is the right thing to do. You've got to stop talking to Denny or Billy. You're going to have to let me make my own decisions.'

'You'll go to prison for something you didn't do!'

'Mum's solicitor says I might not go to prison. He says I've got a good chance of getting community service.'

My mother's solicitor. The words stuck in my ears. My mother had pushed her way back into Brad's life.

'I thought we agreed. I thought we never wanted to see her again!'

'That was a long time ago!'

'But nothing's changed.'

'A lot has changed. I'm in trouble, right?'

'But me and Dad could help.'

Brad shook his head. His cheeks were puffed out. He walked back to the bed and sat beside me.

'I don't want to talk about this any more. You'll just have to let me do it my way.'

He looked away from me and began to pile up his CDs. It was then I looked round and noticed the difference. His room was tidy. There were none of his worn clothes lying around, no scattered magazines, no shoes lying at odd angles. What had happened to make Brad care about such things? It made me feel odd, like an intruder. My brother was changing and it was as if a door had shut between us. He was on one side; I was on the other.

I left him there and went back to my own room.

An hour or so after they had left for the magistrates' court Emily arrived. She looked flushed and hurried and she was carrying a newspaper under her arm.

'I've got something to show you,' she said mysteriously.

She strode ahead into the kitchen and I sloped along behind her.

'The local paper,' she informed me, spreading it out on the kitchen table.

I groaned. I didn't want to see the reports of the accident in black and white.

'Look,' she said, flicking over the pages until she got further into the newspaper.

I stood beside her. At least we were avoiding the headlines. She got to page fifteen and stopped.

'There,' she said, pointing at a small article at the top right-hand corner.

I looked. It was a small piece with no picture. The headline said, **Mobile Phone Theft. Hundreds Stolen in Daring Raid**. I frowned. What did that have to do with anything?

'Read it. Look at the timing!'

Emily was beside herself with excitement. I read the article.

*Thieves staged a daring robbery at PHONEME, in Bush Mall on Sunday between six and seven. Over a hundred of the latest technology mobiles were taken. It is thought that two men hid in the mall toilets just before closing time. When the shopping centre was empty they made their way to the loading bay at the rear and forced their way into the stockroom of the shop. An employee was bound and blindfolded. The robbers escaped with a wide range of the latest mobile phones. CCTV equipment show two hooded males entering the stockroom and leaving some time later. It is understood that the security team were not alerted to this footage until after the crime had taken place. The police urge the public to contact them should they be offered any cheap mobile phones.*

'What has this got to do with anything?' I said.

'This could be the answer,' she said, looking pleased with herself. I was confused. I must have looked weak and hopeless because she said, 'Why don't you sit down and I'll get a cup of tea.'

She talked while she moved round the kitchen.

'At first, you told me that Brad denied being on the footbridge at all. You said he was absolutely certain about that, right? Then he changes his mind. He was there but he never threw the stone, right? Then the driver dies and it all gets more serious. He can't deny it because he said he was there so he just keeps quiet. He gets a solicitor and hopes that they'll get him off or at the very worst he'll be charged with Criminal Damage.'

I sat listening. There was a mug of tea in front of me. I hadn't remembered saying I wanted one. Emily sat opposite me, her eyes glittering.

'I think I know why Brad would confess to something he hadn't done!'

'Why?' I said.

'Because at the time of that road accident he was doing something much worse!'

Emily pointed to the newspaper. I looked down. The article stared back at me. My brother had always loved mobile phones. He had had one before almost anyone else. He knew every feature, every function, every model, every tariff. He held them tenderly and looked after them with great care. He loved them so much he even stole them from people.

'You think he might have done this robbery?'

Emily nodded. She looked pleased with herself, like she'd just got an 'A' on an essay. For a second I hated her. For being squeaky clean. For not having a brother who was in trouble.

'You think a robbery is a worse crime than causing a major traffic accident where a man dies?'

'Yes, but. . .' Emily sat forward with glee '. . . at the time that Brad confessed he didn't know that anyone had died, did he? He just thought that an accident had been caused, damage to cars, some minor injuries, that stuff. When he was accused with this he might have thought to himself, Why not? At least the police can't charge me with the robbery!'

'But how could a robbery be a more important crime than a car crash?' I said, exasperated that she couldn't see my point.

'It is though. Crimes against property are punished more severely than crimes against people. Robbery is a very serious crime. Especially as it was *aggravated*. Meaning they tied the employee up.'

'I know what *aggravated* means!' I snapped.

'Right.'

Emily's face sagged a little. It was dawning on her that I wasn't at all pleased with her Sherlock Holmes act.

'I was just trying to help,' she shrugged.

I looked down at the article and back at her.

'So, now he's saying he did one thing because he doesn't want to say he did this?'

'There's only one way to find out,' Emily said. 'Search his room, his stuff, his car even. See if you can find any evidence.'

'What evidence?'

'Mobile phones.'

'There are loads of mobiles in Brad's room.'

'But not brand spanking new ones.'

'He'd hide them. If they're stolen, he'd hide them!'

'Yeah, but you know Brad's not that bright. He's bound to leave some incriminating evidence behind!'

I huffed. 'Don't say that about Brad. You don't know him. He is bright. He is intelligent. Just because he ignores you there's no need to say untrue things about him.'

Emily stiffened. She began to turn the pages of the newspaper back towards the front. The conversation hadn't gone the way she had wanted it to go.

'He is bright,' I repeated. 'Just because he didn't get good results in his exams . . .'

'It's nothing to do with exams!' Emily said, her voice louder. 'It's that he's the one who always gets caught. Look at Dennis Scott and all the stuff he's done. He never gets caught. But Brad? He's only got to drop a crisp bag in the wrong place and the police are after him. Look at him now. He's owned up to doing something he didn't even do. That's not very bright, is it?'

'You should go, Emily,' I said, standing up. 'I'll ring you later.'

She pursed her lips and looked awkward.

'Look I'm sorry,' she said. 'I didn't mean to . . . I was only trying to help.'

'I know you mean well,' I said, still angry. 'I'm just a bit . . . I can't think straight at the moment. I'll ring you later when Brad gets back from court.'

She stood still for a moment looking perplexed.

'Shall I take the paper?'

'No, it's fine. Leave it here. I'll have a look at it later,' I said, dismissively.

'Take no notice of what I said. It's probably rubbish.'

I nodded.

After she'd gone home I sat down at the kitchen table and looked at the newspaper she had left behind. My heart sank. There it was, front page news. **Road Death. One Family's Loss.** I started to read and realized immediately that it wasn't about the motorway crash. It was the other accident, the one that Emily had read out from the internet news. I was about to look inside the paper when I noticed the photographs. It was a hit-and-run that had involved a child. A sweet-faced little girl was standing posing in a ballet tutu, her hands crossed in front of her, one leg pointed outwards. Beside this was a picture of a car, a silver BMW, which the police were looking for.

The phone rang. I walked out to the hall and picked up the receiver.

'The case was supposed to start about eleven,' my dad said, 'but there's been some legal arguments so it won't actually start until this afternoon. The three of us will have some lunch and I'll ring you if I have any news.'

I replaced the receiver and thought of the three of them having lunch somewhere. My mother sitting opposite my dad and Brad. Maybe people in the cafe would just see them as a regular family. They wouldn't know that I wasn't there.

I walked smartly back into the kitchen. I didn't sit down.

I roughly thumbed the newspaper pages. It wasn't until page eight that I saw a small black frame halfway down: **Lorry Driver Dies After Motorway Pile-Up**. The report was about ten lines long. Easy to miss.

It was eleven-thirty. It would be hours until my dad and Brad came home. Hours before I knew what had happened in the magistrates' court. I began to think about Emily's theory and I turned back to the page about the mobile phone theft.

# 23

Brad's room was in darkness even though it was late morning. He'd pulled down his venetian blind before he'd left for court. I twisted the plastic rod at the side to let some light in. Lines of sun lay across the floor and the bed, making it seem as if I was in a strange place. Somewhere I'd never been before.

And it was spick and span.

The previous night Brad had been tidying up and it had surprised me and made me feel uncomfortable; as though my brother was becoming a different person. Now there wasn't a thing out of place. Not so much as a magazine lying sideways across his bedside table. There wasn't even a hum from his computer; for once he'd turned it off. The room was as quiet as a church. As if no one lived in it.

Why was I there? Because in the hour or so since Emily had gone home I realized that she had put a spark of hope into my head and I wanted to find out if it was true. Robbery is only more serious than a man losing his life in the eyes of the law. I *wanted* Brad to be somewhere else, maybe even in the stockrooms of a mobile phone shop, loading a bag with the latest technology; even tying a man up. Anything was better than being responsible for someone dying.

I started with his desk drawers. They were full of the usual junk: packets of cigarette papers, specks of tobacco (and dope), the tops of filter cigarettes, packets of Polos, chewing-gum, coins. There were old football tickets and lottery slips. Each drawer was just like the next apart from the odd computer disk or CD-ROM. I walked across to his rail of clothes. His second suit was hanging up as well as some dark trousers. A few shirts were ironed and on the end was a tie holder that I had bought him one Christmas. One tie hung forlornly on it, the others flicked over the rail like bunting. Underneath were his other pair of smart shoes lined up with four or five pairs of trainers.

His bed was made, the duvet neatly puffed up. I didn't bother to look underneath. I cast my eye over his bookshelves, his true crime books. They were straight and neat. When had he done this? Why?

It dawned on me. He'd cleared his room up because he thought he might not be coming back to it. He thought he might be taken into custody. I felt this flash of anguish for him. What about all the bravado? My mother's solicitor was going to get him off with community service. Did he say that just to make me feel better?

I opened his bedside drawer and was surprised to see a packet of condoms. It made me smile for a moment. I thought of my brother in a lot of ways but I never thought of him as someone's boyfriend, someone's lover.

It made me think of Denny and I sat down on the bed.

Denny had been here, in Brad's room, a couple of nights before. *If you're gonna confess you do it yourself, don't pull me in*, he'd said, his voice low and urgent. Whatever had happened they had been together. Brad and Denny, long-term mates, loyal to each other. Partners in crime.

And me and Denny? Would I see him again? He hadn't lied. He'd told the truth when he said he wasn't on the footbridge. It was a small crumb of honesty that hid something big, something neither he nor my brother wanted anyone to know about.

I looked back at my brother's drawer. Full of rubbish, bottle tops, pens, empty deodorants, screwed-up paper, a key ring and some money. I closed it.

My shoulders sagged. What was I doing there? Brad and Denny would hold their secret tightly between them. I lay back on his bed and turned my face into his pillow. There was a strong scent of tobacco and sweat. When I was young my brother always used to smell of sweets: sherbet, cola drops, chocolate buttons or strawberry Fruitellas. Now he smelt like a man: beery and smoky. What did Denny smell of? I closed my eyes and tried to remember. His body always seemed so hot, so fiery. I thought of my face buried in his neck breathing in the scent of spearmint and hair shampoo. Sometimes, when he rolled over on to me my senses closed and I could only feel his fingers on my skin. I screwed up the corners of Brad's pillow. Why wasn't Denny straightforward? Why hadn't he asked me to be his girlfriend? Why did everything I think of always travel back to him?

I sat up and thought for a minute. Then I pulled open Brad's bedside drawer and looked. Denny; always, always, everything led back to him. There were no state-of-the-art mobile phones in my brother's room. No packaging, no clues as to whether or not he had taken part in the robbery. There was one thing though. I fished out the key ring. A single key hanging from a brass ring attached to a skull key fob. Exactly the same as the one Denny had. It opened a lock-up garage on the Waterways estate where Denny said he kept some spare parts for his car.

Was that garage full of stolen mobile phones?

I sighed. Then I went and phoned Emily.

# 24

We had to wait on buses but we finally got to the estate around two. Emily had brought a couple of rolls with her and some cartons of orange. We ate them on the bus. It was as if we were on some odd sort of picnic; our previous awkwardness gone now that we were together in something. She was looking for evidence of my brother's guilt and I was looking for evidence of his innocence.

We came to the place where Denny had stopped his car while he got out and went to his lock-up garage. In my pocket was the key with the skull's head. Emily had got a good look at it. *I wonder if the skull symbolizes anything?* she'd said. I didn't answer. I finished my drink and looked for a bin to put the carton in.

'No litter bins anywhere,' Emily said. 'No wonder these estates are such a mess.'

A couple of girls walked by. They were from our school but they were not the kind who mixed with us. They wore the minimum amount of clothes, their breasts stuck out defiantly and their honey-coloured midriffs each flashed with a glittering navel jewel. They were heavily made up, their black eyelashes like tiny brushes. They ignored us. I suddenly envied them. They had no worries. They were gliding along the street probably looking for lads. Maybe they'd find some and spend the afternoon in a dark bedroom somewhere. The thought of it made my skin tingle.

'Look at those Year Tens. Don't they look cheap!' Emily said.

'It's this way,' I said, heading for the newsagent's.

We walked across the street. I put my empty drink carton into a bin. We went down the short alleyway to a line of three garages, two quite big and the third smaller. The end one was one of the larger ones and we crossed to it. I had the key ready but we had to wait because there was a tiny van making its way along the back of the shops. The driver had his hazard lights flashing on and off. He was edging around a couple of parked motorbikes so we stood until he passed us and went up the alleyway on to the street.

I was nervous. If the garage was stacked with mobile phone boxes I would know that Brad had been involved in a robbery. It would mean that he hadn't been on the footbridge, causing a man's death. I *wanted* Emily to be right. There was a prickle of apprehension in my chest. I needed to know. Emily put her hand out for the key and I gave it to her. She put it in the lock and fiddled with it for a moment.

'Come on,' Emily said to the key, impatient.

Her expression was one of concentration. Her eyes were glowing, her hair curling over her shoulder. There was a springiness about her. It depressed me. This was an *adventure* to her.

The key turned and she pulled one of the doors open. I stepped forward. I expected to be faced with a wall of mobile phone boxes but it was dark. Emily walked in.

'There's a car in here,' she said.

'It is a garage,' I said stepping after her, careful where I put my foot in the dark, small space.

'There's a light just over here,' she said.

A moment or two later an electric light came on, illuminating the garage. There was a car, covered with a variety of old sheets. In the corner were tools, piled up on top of each other. There was a smell about the place: oil, petrol, detergent. I scanned the walls, looking for cupboards or shelves. Anything which might have held boxes of mobile phones. There were none. It was just a greasy, grimy garage. I felt myself sag with disappointment. Emily hadn't said a word. She'd stopped looking and was fussing over the car, lifting the sheets off its bonnet.

'What?' I said.

She looked up at me, her face more serious than it had been all day.

'I don't know,' she said. 'I could be wrong . . .'

'What?' I said, louder, more impatient, feeling that I had a right to be miffed.

'It's a silver BMW and the front is smashed up a bit.'

'So?' I said.

'Dennis Scott's car is red, isn't it? And Brad's . . .'

'Brad's is black. So what?'

'What's this car doing here?'

'Maybe it's not Denny's. Maybe he's doing some work on it for someone else! What does it matter?'

'Because it's smashed up. As if it hit something. A bus stop. That's what it said in the paper.'

'Paper?'

'Did you bring it with you? The newspaper I brought to your house?'

I was exasperated.

'Do I look like I've got the newspaper?' I said, holding my arms out as if it was hidden somewhere on my person.

'I don't know if you read it. Or noticed in the news this week. You've probably been too preoccupied.'

'Will you tell me what you're talking about!' I said.

Emily pulled the sheet off the front of the car. I stepped across. It was silver and looked newer than Denny's other car. It did have a dent on the front passenger side wing and light.

'The hit-and-run. A little girl got hit. She died. The report said that the police were looking for a silver BMW.'

She looked at me. Her eyebrows were twitching as though she was trying to work something out.

'But what's it doing here?' she said, lower, as if she was speaking to herself, as if I wasn't there at all.

It was then that the awful truth hit me. She was skirting around it. Maybe she even knew, guessed the moment she lifted the sheet up off the car. The silver BMW. The girl in the tutu and ballet shoes. She'd been hit by a car that hadn't stopped. This car. Hidden in Denny's lock-up. We'd been looking for stolen phones but we'd found something much much worse.

'Brad and Denny were driving this car, on Sunday evening,' I said.

'They hit the girl and drove off,' Emily said, uncertainly. 'It wasn't meant, I'm sure. It was an accident . . .'

'They killed a little girl!' I said.

'That's why Brad admitted to being on the footbridge. If he was there then he couldn't have been in this car!' Emily said.

Her previous carefree attitude had gone. She looked crestfallen. She had been proved right. Brad had admitted guilt to avoid being accused of something much worse. A hit-and-run. Two lads in a car, careering along a road and taking a tiny ballerina with them. I felt myself lean forward, my elbows on the hood of the damaged BMW. Denny and Brad, always together in everything they did.

'What shall we do?' Emily said.

I had no answer.

# Saturday

## 25

Tony Haskins wasn't due in to work on Saturday morning but he went into the station anyway. He had some paperwork to do. Not that you could really call it *paper*work any more, he thought, sitting down at the computer screen, using the mouse to access the files he wanted. These days it was more like *machine* work. He was a machine operator, putting information into a keyboard and watching as it was sucked into a square box on his screen. At the press of a button he could make it all appear again.

If only it was like that with people. If it was as cut and dried as that. You pressed a button and they told you everything they knew. But it wasn't.

He accessed the *Paul Sullivan* file. There were several security steps he had to go through and he looked round the office while his fingers automatically typed the required passwords and security clearance data. The only other person there was Dom Kennedy. He was at the far desk peering into a computer screen. He was probably doing the exact same thing. Keeping his paperwork (computer files) up to date. No doubt he was still working on the hit-and-run. Tony's screen cleared and his case papers appeared. He began to fill in the unfinished sections. He did it automatically, hardly needing to think about his actions.

The previous day he'd been in the magistrates' court as Bradley Simon had had his first hearing. The lad had pleaded *Not Guilty* to Manslaughter. His solicitor had asked for an adjournment and it had been granted. Bradley was given the usual bail restrictions and the family went off home.

In the courtroom, waiting for the case to start, Lee Simon had called Tony over and introduced him to his ex-wife and another young lad. *This is Sally, Brad's mum, and Dennis Scott, here, is Brad's mate. We've come to give him moral support.*

The young lad, Dennis, had looked familiar. Or maybe, Tony thought, running his fingers across his scalp, all young people started to look the same as you got older.

Bradley's mother's presence had been a surprise. A smart woman with short wavy hair, she looked younger than Lee, as if she was from a different generation. She had a slim pad, he remembered, and was poised to take notes. It had hardly been worth her getting it out; the case was quickly dealt with and pushed forward for three weeks.

Afterwards, he'd walked out of the court and into the wide corridor and seen the group of them by one of the benches. Bradley was seated next to the other young lad, Dennis, and his father and mother were standing talking. Brad had taken his tie off and was pulling at the collar of his shirt as if it was suffocating him. His friend was grinning, talking close to Brad's ear. When he saw Tony approach he stiffened and pulled back, taking a piece of gum out of a packet and popping it into his mouth like a pill. Tony again had the feeling that he knew him from somewhere but then that wasn't surprising. When he'd been a PC he'd had a lot of contact with teenage boys. Maybe this lad was just another of those.

'Tea?'

A voice interrupted his thoughts. It was Dom, standing with a steaming mug. Tony hadn't even noticed him getting up to make it. He accepted the drink and sat back from his computer. Dom pulled out a nearby chair, sat on it and sighed.

'Still looking for the car in the hit-and-run?' Tony said.

Dom nodded. 'You know how many silver BMWs there are in this area?'

'Hundreds?'

'More. Much more. We can't check them all, not with the manpower issue. We're hoping that someone will grass up the driver. What with it being a little girl who died . . .'

'Maybe it's hidden away somewhere? In a garage?'

'Sure. But still, if it was used someone might have noticed. A neighbour, a friend, a colleague. Someone might have noticed that a silver BMW that was recently in use is no longer around.'

'Any help with the other witness, the friend?'

Kennedy shook his head. 'Just a big silver car that came up on the pavement, hit the bus shelter and her friend and then drove off. Poor little mite. It's probably better that she doesn't remember much about it.'

'No other new witnesses?'

'One, yesterday. Elizabeth Bell, likes to be called Lizzie. She lives in a street off the high road. On Sunday evening she'd just driven back from the airport – two weeks in Crete – and was unloading her suitcases from her car. A car screeched round the corner and pulled up for a moment double-parking. It was silver. She's not sure what type.'

Tony nodded.

'You know how many silver cars there are in this area? You don't want to know. Thousands. Anyway it sat there for a moment and somebody got out of the passenger seat and ran back up towards the main road. She was tired so she didn't hang around. She went to bed and slept and spent the next few days getting back to work, back into her routine, and didn't register the news. That's why she only came forward yesterday after reading the story in the local paper.'

'She say anything about the person who got out of the car?'

'Young, white, male. That was all.'

'Um . . .' Tony drank his tea.

'You know how many young white males there are in this area?'

'I don't want to know,' Tony Haskins said. Kennedy gave a wry smile and got up, taking Tony's cup from him even though he hadn't quite finished his tea. Tony turned back to the computer and finished his work.

Later, when he was walking towards his car he remembered when he'd seen Bradley Simon's mate, Dennis. About five or six months before, he'd come in early one day to get ready for a conference on Street Crime. He'd been walking past the holding cells and seen Bradley, looking worse for wear, standing in front of the duty sergeant. The lad's hair was sticking up and there was a strong smell of booze coming from him. He'd sighed. Bradley Simon seemed to love the inside of the police station. He didn't bother to speak to him. He could hear the sergeant reminding him of the terms of his caution and then listing out his belongings.

A few moments later Tony had gone outside for a breath of fresh air. A whole day listening to speaker after speaker was going to be a trial. He'd walked across the road from the station to a newsagent's and bought several goodies to see him through the sessions: a carton of Ribena, a packet of mints and some wine gums. Heading back he saw a car pull up right across the exit from the station car park. The driver got out and stood there cheekily, talking on his mobile phone, as if daring someone to come out and book him. Then Bradley Simon came out and grinned at the driver. Tony watched as Bradley got in and the other boy walked back to the driver's door. He made eye contact with Tony, just for a second, no more. Then he got in. It was Dennis Scott, Bradley's mate.

And the car was a silver BMW.

He remembered thinking at the time, *How can a kid of that age afford a car like that?* If it had been Bradley's he would definitely have investigated further. But it wasn't and he forgot about it.

A silver BMW.

Tony stopped abruptly, did an about-turn and went back into the station and up the stairs to the office. He wondered if Dom was still there. He was, facing his computer. Tony picked up the kettle and refilled it. This time he was going to make the tea.

# 26

I woke up about eight. I had a furry mouth and a headache. I looked around and remembered where I was. In Emily's bedroom, on the fold-down spare bed, looking across at Emily sleeping.

On the floor, on a tray, were two empty bottles of wine and a couple of plates and bowls. Had we drunk all of that? *Have a glass*, Emily had said, *it will make you feel better*. It had. For a few hours we left the untidy subject of the silver car behind us in the garage on the Waterways estate. My brother and Denny driving away from a tiny ballerina who had pirouetted on to the road in front of them. Was that how it had happened? We'd talked it over and over until we were exhausted. *Stay over*, Emily had said. *You can decide what to do tomorrow.*

Why go home? I thought. My dad had sent me a text to say that Brad's case had been adjourned for three weeks. No doubt my mother would be there giving her opinion, pushing her way further back into our house, into our lives. I sent a text back to say that I was going to stay at Emily's and that I'd see them the next day.

I sat up, my head feeling heavy, like a bowling ball. I was thirsty and needed to go to the toilet. I stood up slowly and looked round for something to put over my underwear. Emily's dressing-gown was on one of the new hooks she'd bought from IKEA. I put it on and went out to the bathroom.

After three cupped handfuls of cold tap water I looked at myself in the mirror. My hair was sticking out at the side from where I'd been lying on it. My eyelids looked heavy and my skin pale. My lips were still parched. I was a mess. I took my clothes off and stepped into the shower and stood under the water for a while. I washed myself thoroughly, scrubbing my skin hard, wetting my hair, letting the water soak through me.

After drying myself I crept back into Emily's bedroom. From downstairs I could hear a radio. Emily's mum in the kitchen, perhaps. I looked for my clothes and slipped them on. Emily was still sound asleep, her mouth making little gurgling noises every time she exhaled. I hung her dressing-gown back up and went out of the room and downstairs.

'Hello, Charlie!' Mrs Little said, standing at the kitchen door wearing an apron covered in rabbits.

'Hi,' my voice crackled.

A smell of baking was wafting from the kitchen. It was bread. Emily's mum baked her own bread! Any other day I would have been impressed. That day it made me feel mildly nauseous.

'Will you have some breakfast?' she said.

'I've got to go, see Brad,' I said.

She nodded, understandingly.

'I could give you a lift?' she said.

'No, I'll get the bus. I need the fresh air.'

I left her house and walked to the bus stop. The cool morning air brushed past my face making me feel a bit better. I leaned against the stop and looked at the cars passing. There was no sign of a bus. I sighed and walked over to a garden wall and sat down.

What was I going to do?

I now knew that my brother and Denny had something to do with the hit-and-run. *Something to do with . . .* This was the phrase Emily and I had used when we were talking about it the previous evening. It was a nice form of words and avoided the actual truth of the matter. They were driving in the silver car and ran over a little girl. They drove off without bothering to stop and see if they could help. Maybe they had been going too fast? Or drinking? Or high on drugs? Whatever. They had left her there, lying in the road. They had sped off, a trail of exhaust fumes hanging in the air behind them and a girl who would never dance again. *Maybe they panicked?* Emily had said, trying to find a way to make me feel better. Now that my brother was definitely guilty of something awful Emily was trying to find excuses for him.

A bus arrived. I hadn't even noticed it coming. I got on and sat at the back near a window which I opened. The air blew in at my face. A beep sounded from my bag. I rummaged around and found my mobile. I had a text message. I pressed the button and saw the words *Need to see you. Denny XXXXX*

I looked at it for a while, my mouth closed in a straight

line. In spite of a feeling of indignation I felt my chest go weak. Even now, even after what I knew about him, his lies and his guilt, I still wanted him. He was unfaithful and untrustworthy and in the end he was bad. But my stomach burned and my skin rippled when I thought of being with him.

What was I going to do?

I put the mobile back in bag, felt around and found the key with the skull fob. *Is the skull symbolic?* Emily had said in her 'A' level English Literature student mode and I had rolled my eyes. But it had been symbolic after all. A symbol of death.

Both accidents had happened at almost the same time. The motorway crash a little after seven. The hit-and-run a little before. Emily and I had bought another copy of the local newspaper and we'd checked it on the web. Little wonder that Brad had owned up to throwing a stone off a motorway footbridge. How much more preferable was that to owning up to hitting a child and leaving her there. He had never expected the driver to die. No one had. Maybe Denny had advised him. *You admit to being there, they can't pin the hit-and-run on you. You can't be in two places at once!* And Denny? He hadn't needed to own up to anything. His week had been completely normal, blowing hot and cold with Tania and playing round with me whenever he had a free moment.

Like now. I got my mobile out and looked at the screen again. *Need to see you.* What for? Silly question. I knew exactly what he wanted to see me for. It wasn't *Love*. I was never going to be his girlfriend. He wanted to be my teacher. I was to be his willing pupil. Just the thought of it made me twist and turn in my seat. Why shouldn't I see him? I looked at the key, at the skull. Then I looked back to the mobile and felt my hands go limp. Of course I would go and see him.

But it would be the last time.

# 27

Denny took a few minutes to open his front door. When he appeared he was wearing boxer shorts, nothing else. His skin was damp as if he'd just stepped out of the shower. I walked past him, keen to get in off the street. I stopped in the hallway and looked towards the kitchen. He read my thoughts.

'Mum's out. Dad too. I'm all alone!'

He held his hands out in a childish way. His face was mischievous. As if we were about to play a game of trains or Lego.

'Let's go upstairs,' I said, licking my dry lips.

I went ahead of him. Steam and the smell of smoke wafted out of the bathroom door. I walked into his bedroom. His bed was unmade and a towel was hanging over the back of a chair. There were some clean clothes laid out on the seat of the chair, waiting for him to dress. I sat on the bed and put my bag on the floor.

'You wanted to see me,' I said.

'I did,' he answered, sitting down beside me. 'I just didn't think you'd come so soon.'

'What for?' I sat, turning sideways, looking straight at his dark eyes, his wet hair.

'To see if you were all right. After yesterday, the court case. I know you were worried about it.'

'Yeah,' I said, shrugging my shoulders. 'But you were right all along. It'll probably be fine.'

I put a hand on his chest and leaned across and kissed him. His skin was hot and he tasted of toothpaste. After a moment's hesitation he seemed to rear up and started to kiss me back. His arm circled my shoulders and his fingers held my forearm tightly. His other hand was pulling at the bottom of my T-shirt.

My eyes were closed and I was lost in the kiss. I didn't want it to end. My head felt heavy, as if I needed to lie down. I began to fall backwards and felt him pull at my hand and drag it towards his boxers. My eyes opened. This was how it always was. Denny taught me things that made him happy, that gave him pleasure. Now it was my turn. I pulled myself up off the bed. He was lying back on one elbow watching me, a tiny smirk on his lips. He thought I was fighting with myself, trying to be a good girl. He liked it when I did that. Then he would have to persuade me all over again. But that wasn't why I was standing up.

I unzipped my jeans and took my T-shirt off. Then I pulled off my bra and pants. I stood naked before him with my boy's body. I wasn't ashamed. Why should I care what he thought? He wasn't someone to admire. I stood proud, holding his stare. I wanted him. I was tired of all the playing about. He looked startled and sat up.

'What?' he said, mildly embarrassed. He hadn't expected the game to go the whole distance.

'Have you got a condom?' I said, my voice heavy.

He nodded. He seemed to shudder and leaned towards me. He placed a hand on each side of my hips and kissed my stomach. Then he pulled me back on to the bed. Lying on my side, facing him, there was a long, hungry kiss and I felt my skin rise up and my blood race round my body. He pulled back for a moment and leaned across to his bedside table, fumbling about in the drawer. I had my head flat on the bed and my eyes closed. I could feel the rumpled duvet underneath me and I could hear the sound of a wrapper being torn. In moments he was back beside me and then on top of me. I was holding him tightly, my fingers digging hard into his skin. For that moment he was mine. It was what I'd wanted for a long time. A moment's tension, a few seconds where his body stiffened and then he seemed to fall from a great height, a moan coming from him as his mouth sank into my shoulder.

I shivered and after a few moments I gently pushed him away. I stood up, my back to him. I pulled my clothes on and went out to the toilet. Washing my face I looked into the mirror. There was no satisfaction there. No great change. Had I expected to look different? Older? Wiser? Instead my hair was messed up and my skin a little red. I was still Charlie Simon. Never been kissed. At least not by someone who cared about me.

I went back into his room. He had dressed and was sitting on the chair, one leg resting on the bed, putting his socks on. He was looking pleased with himself. My visit had been a bonus for him.

I went straight over to my bag. All of a sudden I felt nervous, my fingers fiddling with the catch, my wrist trembling as I rummaged inside for the key. I found it and held it up, its skull's head hanging ludicrously like something from a game of pirates. I swallowed and said the words I had decided on earlier.

'I know about the silver BMW. I know the police are looking for it. I know it's in your garage.'

He looked puzzled for a moment. Then worried.

'Hang on,' he said. 'What are you talking about?'

'The car you keep in your lock-up? It was used in that hit-and-run?'

He shook his head and his face had an expression of incredulity.

'That's why you got Brad to plead guilty. If he was on the motorway footbridge then he couldn't have been in a hit-and-run. You weren't to know that the driver would die.'

'This is stupid,' he said.

But I didn't listen. I looked at his face and I could see his eyes were blank. Before, sitting on the bed, they were deep enough for me to sink into but now they were cold and hard.

'I'm going home to see Brad now.'

'You're going to grass on your brother? You know he'll get real jail time for this. It's much more serious than just throwing a stone. He'll go to prison for years. Years and years.'

There was a catch in Denny's voice. He was troubled, I

could tell. He was leaning forward on the chair, his stockinged feet moving about. He was agitated.

'I'm going home,' I said, taking a step away.

He stood up immediately and blocked my way. He was in front of me, not so tall without his shoes.

'Charlie,' he whispered, 'this is silly. You're going to get us into trouble for no reason. It was an accident. A terrible accident. Nothing you can do now will bring that little girl back.'

He was rubbing his hands lightly up and down my arm. He sounded so soft, so sympathetic.

'My brother shouldn't go to prison for something he hasn't done. He wasn't on that motorway bridge. He needs to tell the truth. So do you.'

Denny's face dropped and his brow wrinkled. His hands tightened on my arms.

'I've got to go.'

'So, what was all that about? On the bed?'

'I was just finishing something off.'

'There was nothing to finish off,' he said, dropping his grip, walking away from me. 'There never was anything. I already have a girlfriend. I was just helping you out. Teaching you a few things.'

'I know,' I said, my voice trembling. 'I always knew. Thanks for the help. I think I can manage without you from now on.'

I walked down the stairs and out of his house. When I closed the door behind me I felt sun on my face. I pictured Denny grabbing his mobile and ringing Brad, getting him ready for my return, for my news. It didn't matter. It was all going to come out one way or another.

I straightened my back and walked off towards the bus stop.

## 28

When I got home I found Brad sitting in the kitchen and my dad cooking bacon. On the side there were four slices of bread ready and buttered and a bottle of brown sauce standing ready.

'Bacon sarnie?' my dad said.

I knew then that Denny hadn't rung Brad.

I looked at my brother. He was wearing his boxer shorts and an old baggy T-shirt, reading the morning paper spread out on the table. He glanced up at me and grunted. It was his usual greeting, a little muted because of the rows we'd had that week.

'I can put a few more slices under the grill?' my dad said, looking jolly, as if everything was all right, as if we hadn't just had our worst week since my mother left home all those years ago.

I shook my head and looked around. The work surface was in a mess. There were crumbs everywhere and the butter was sitting open. I could hear the bacon crackling under the grill and I was sure that my dad hadn't lined the grill pan with tinfoil.

'I'm glad you're home. We can tell you about yesterday. It's all looking quite hopeful. The solicitor says that the police have no real evidence and that Brad's story will be taken seriously precisely because he confessed to being there. With a bit of luck the case will be dismissed . . .'

'I need to say something,' I said, gloomily.

My dad scooped the bacon up with a spatula and turned the grill off. He let the bacon tip on to the bread and made himself busy preparing the sandwiches.

'Fire away,' he said, his back to me.

Brad looked up from the paper.

'What's up?' he said.

I suddenly didn't know where to start. I had this huge thing to say but couldn't find the right words. My dad and Brad were looking expectantly at me, my dad holding a saw knife in midair waiting to cut the sandwiches in half.

'What's up, love?' he said. 'Is it about Mum? I know it's all a bit sudden, her turning up, but maybe . . .'

I shook my head and sat down at the table. I got out the key from my bag and lay it on top of the newspaper that Brad was reading.

'I know about the silver car. And about the hit-and-run.'

My dad plonked two plates on the table and sat down.

'What silver car?' he said cheerfully.

Brad looked at the key for what seemed like a long time. Then he appeared to deflate. His shoulders slumped and his chest fell. He folded his arms across his ribs. My dad had already taken a bite of sandwich and was chewing, looking puzzled. He put the sandwich down and his expression changed.

'Charlie, will you tell me what you're talking about?'

He was looking at me as if I'd done something wrong. How I wished that Denny had rung and told Brad before I got there. Instead he had left it to me. How typical of Denny. He never seemed to get his hands dirty, not even when it came to warning his best mate.

'Denny and Brad were in a car that hit a little girl. *Killed* a little girl.'

'What?'

'Tell him, Brad. It's true, isn't it?'

Brad leaned forward dramatically, his forehead touching the edge of the table. Then he raised his head a couple of centimetres and slammed it back on to the wooden surface; once, twice, three times. I stood up in shock. My dad shouted out, threw his chair back and stepped across, grabbing hold of Brad to stop him. Brad kept rocking though, his shoulders going back and forth, a low moan coming from him.

'Stop it,' my dad said, holding Brad's head in the crook of his arm. 'Stop it. STOP IT!'

There was blood near Brad's eye; it ran down the side of his face, crimson . . . Brad started to shiver, a great hiccupping sob coming from him.

'Brad, son, what's this about?'

My dad was holding Brad's face, looking sternly at me.

'We did,' Brad said, stuttering. 'We hit her. She was at a bus stop. The car veered. We weren't even going fast. But we had some cans of beer and Denny was smoking dope. It was horrible. It was horrible . . .'

'Charlie. Explain. Now.'

'Brad wasn't on the motorway footbridge last Sunday evening. He was driving around with Denny Scott in a silver BMW. It hit a little girl. They didn't stop, they just drove off. She's dead. The girl is dead.'

My throat dried up and I felt my eyes glossing over. They were just words but they meant so much. The dead schoolgirl. Brad and Denny driving away.

'Oh my God,' my dad said, moving back, away from Brad, putting his hands behind him to lean on the work surface. 'Oh good God, what have you done!'

Brad stood up. He looked pathetic. He used the back of his hand to wipe the blood from his cheek and smeared it across his face. His T-shirt was grubby and his boxers ragged at the ends.

'I wanted to stop. I told Denny to stop. I got out and ran back but it was too late. She was lying on the road, other people around. It was too late.'

My dad's face had a look of bewilderment on it.

'But the motorway crash?' he said.

'Denny said it would be better for me to be charged with that than banged up for this. We didn't know that the driver was going to die. We didn't know!'

There was a touch of pique in Brad's voice as though he was annoyed at the driver for thwarting his plan.

'You were trying to save your skin?' my dad cried. 'You weren't even worried about the little girl, you were just looking after yourself.'

'I wanted to go back but Denny said, with my record, with my luck, it would get blamed on me.'

'You were drinking cans of beer and driving?'

'No, no! I wasn't driving! Denny was driving. He was smoking dope. I was drinking. I'd been drinking all afternoon. I was pissed. I don't even remember driving along the high road. I just heard the bang when we hit the bus stop and the girl.'

Brad hadn't been driving. I felt a weight lift off my shoulders. I'd thought he had been. Why? What had made me think that? There was trouble and I assumed that he had been the one to cause it. Wasn't that always the way? But Brad had been a passenger. *He'd been drinking but he wasn't the driver!*

My dad must have been thinking the same thing.

'But how could you be banged up for anything? You weren't even driving!'

'Denny said, with my record . . .' He left the words hanging.

'He drove away. *Denny* drove away,' I said.

'I was drunk! Denny said I knocked against him. I made him swerve.'

'But you weren't driving!' I said.

I'd begun to rub my arms with my hands. Denny had been smoking. He'd sat holding a joint with one hand and the steering wheel with the other. Maybe he brought it up to his lips at the moment he saw the girl, too late to turn away, too late to put the brake on. I turned away from my dad and my brother. My eyes closed, I thought of myself an hour earlier, lying among his mussed-up bedclothes. Drinking him in, desiring him, needing him on top of me, to finish it all. He had lied and lied and still I had wanted him.

'Charlie, where you going?'

My dad's voice followed me out of the room and then I let the door shut and went upstairs.

My mother came about an hour later. I stood at the door of my room and listened. Her voice was soft, her words calm. My dad spoke rapidly, his words careering into one another, and Brad hardly spoke at all, just a low mumble. The sound muted as the living-room door shut behind them. Not long after there were phone calls. My dad talking to someone, perhaps the solicitor, possibly Max Robbins.

Eventually I closed the door of my room and lay on my bed. Not long afterwards there was a knock. I stiffened, thinking it was my mother, but it wasn't. The door opened and Brad stood there. He'd put some jeans and a T-shirt on and his forehead had been cleaned up.

'All right to come in?' he said sheepishly.

He sat down on the bed beside me. I didn't say anything to him because I honestly didn't know what to say. He was stupid, idiotic. He'd got himself in an awful mess and for once it didn't even look as though it was his fault.

'Charlie, I've been a prat. I panicked. I wasn't thinking straight.'

'You lied to *me*,' I said.

'How could I tell you about *this*? How could I? I know it looks bad. I know he thinks I'm a complete nutter,' he said, pointing down to the floor.

I couldn't answer. I was fed up trying to build bridges between him and my dad.

'That's why, when Mum showed up . . .' He shrugged. 'She didn't think I was all bad . . .'

I stiffened. My mother was not part of this, not in my eyes.

'Whose car is it?' I interrupted.

'Me and Denny, we bought it together. It's old but top range. It's not insured, see, so we only use it now and then. We've had it for nearly a year. Sometimes I drive it. Sometimes he does. We share it. It stays in his lock-up.'

I could hear noises from downstairs. The sound of the telephone ringing and my dad answering it. He called my mum's name and then I could hear her voice. I wondered if it was my dad's brother ringing up and asking to speak to his *wife*.

'I want to tell you what happened,' he said.

'What? The truth? Only I've heard a number of stories from you this week.'

'Swear. This is the truth. Last Sunday I was out with Billy Warner and some other mates. We were at the pub near High Beech. My car was parked there but I wasn't fit to drive it. About six Denny drives up in the BM. I get in and toss my keys to Billy and go off with Denny.'

Billy Warner. He must have driven Brad's car to the lane near the footbridge. Him and some others. That's why Brad was picked up in the first place.

'Denny's had some beers and stuff and we drove around for a while, drinking, talking. We even saw some girls down by the multiplex off the A13. Denny said, *Let's see if we can't get them in the car. Give them a ride.* It's no good though. The blonde one likes Denny. They all do. Her mate won't come though. So we drove off. Denny had a joint. If only those girls had got in. Everything would have been different.'

In the middle of this story there was another bitter pill. Denny had been with me in the late afternoon. We lay on the floor of my living-room playing with each other, making each other hot and bothered. Then, a couple of hours later Denny was hungry again, trying to pick up girls. Girls were fast food for Denny.

'We were driving for a while and then out of the blue Denny seemed to lose control. The car hit a kerb. I don't remember exactly, there was just this big bump and we scraped along the side of a bus stop. At first I thought that was it. I was kind of laughing, you know. But Denny was swearing and pulling at the steering wheel so that we could get away and I looked round and I saw her, this little girl lying in the road.'

From downstairs I could hear the sound of the front door bell ringing. I looked at Brad. His face had reddened and he was picking at the skin around his fingernails.

'I told Denny to stop. But he drove on. He turned round the first corner and I opened the door so he had to stop. He did and I got out and ran back to look. There was a group of people around her and other people running from far away. I just panicked, got back in the car and we drove off, back to the lock-up.'

'You have to go to the police,' I said. 'Tell them the truth.'

Brad was nodding but it was half-hearted.

'You have to tell them that Denny was driving. You are not to blame for this!' I said.

There was noise from downstairs. Male voices were talking in the hallway. I could hear Dad calling for Brad.

We got up and walked out to the landing. Brad swore under his breath.

We could see a police officer standing in the hallway downstairs. Beside him was Tony Haskins. My dad was there and my mother was standing by them talking into a mobile phone. She was saying, *You have to come, George, it's important* . . .

Brad paused for a minute. Then he went towards them. I followed. My mum cut her call and then they were all standing in the tiny hallway looking awkward. I stood beside Brad, as far away from my mother as it was possible to stand.

'Brad and me were just about to come down to the station,' my dad was saying. 'He has some information . . .'

Tony Haskins shook his head as if to silence my dad.

'It's too late, Lee. We've just had a young man and his solicitor in the station. He says he was a passenger in a car which was driven by Bradley Simon. This car hit and killed Katie Swallow, last Sunday evening at just before seven o'clock. I have to take Bradley in now. I suggest you sort a solicitor out pronto.'

'Who said that? Denny said that? No. *Denny* wouldn't say that.'

Brad's voice was tiny. He looked around at everyone.

'You have to come now, Bradley,' Tony Haskins said, holding his arm out as if he was about to open the door for Brad.

'Denny wouldn't say that!'

Tony Haskins sighed.

'He says you killed the little girl and refused to stop. He says you threatened him with physical violence and that's why he hasn't come forward until now. This doesn't look good for you, Bradley.'

Brad seemed to harden. I felt his body become heavy and rigid. I put my hand on his arm. There was the slightest tremble.

'I'll come, Brad. I can be a witness.'

But he shook me off.

'It's OK,' he said, looking straight at Tony Haskins, 'I'll tell you what happened. I'll tell you all of it.'

The front door opened and they took him out. My dad picked up his jacket from the banister and followed them. My mother got her car keys out, rattling them efficiently.

'Do you want to come in my car?' she said.

I shook my head and went back upstairs.

# Sunday

## 29

Tony and Dom sat on one side of the desk in the office of their boss. Jimmy Kilmartin was a family man and didn't like coming into work on a Sunday morning. He had a red, white and blue checked short-sleeved shirt on and some casual trousers. He looked out of place, awkward. He spent some moments lining up some framed photographs of his family. His car keys sat on the table as if ready for a quick escape.

'Good work,' he said gruffly, taking a swig from a mug of tea. 'Where are our two reprobates?'

He was always using old-fashioned words like that: *reprobates, miscreants, scoundrels*. He reminded Tony a bit of a head teacher he had once had.

'In the holding cells. Both telling their own stories.'

'No loyalty among crooks.' Jimmy Kilmartin shook his head slowly. 'Both blaming each other?'

'Bradley Simon has a record, mostly to do with stealing and affray. No *driving* offences as such. The other, Dennis Scott, has an unblemished record. Pure as the driven snow. Insists he was an innocent passenger and was then intimidated by Bradley Simon.'

179

'What's your view?'

'Bradley's certainly capable of a lot of things but . . .'

'Tony has a soft spot for Bradley Simon,' Dom said, cheekily.

'No, it's just that . . . Well, I don't think this is the kind of thing I'd put him down for. In the past, when I've talked to him he's almost owned up on the spot!'

'This is more serious . . .'

'But still. It doesn't feel like something Bradley would . . .'

'We've got the witness, Elizabeth Bell, coming in at twelve,' Dom said.

'Any hope there? Did she get a good look at the boy?'

'Hard to say. If she can identify the lad who got out of the passenger side to run back up the road then we'll know that he wasn't the driver.'

'But what are the chances of that?' Dom said. 'Two white boys, similar heights, same colour hair . . .'

'Well, give it a go. I'd like to go home for my Sunday lunch. Roast lamb and mint sauce. My favourite.'

Tony felt his mouth water. Dom shook his head.

'Meat? Not good for the arteries. I'm a vegetarian!'

Elizabeth Bell arrived at twelve. She still had a dark tan from her holiday in Crete. She was quite nice-looking, too. Tony looked down at her ring finger and was pleasantly surprised to see there was no ring and no white mark where one might have been. Dom Kennedy was working on some of Dennis Scott's statement with him so he'd asked Tony to set up the identification.

'If you'd just follow me, Miss Bell,' Tony said.

'Call me Lizzie, please. No need to be formal, that's what I always say!'

Tony showed her into a computer suite and pulled a chair out for her to sit on.

'Will there be an identity parade?' Lizzie said.

'We don't do it like that any more,' Tony smiled.

'I can picture him in my head, you know, but . . .'

'That's fine. You should only point him out if you're absolutely sure.'

Tony sat down at the next desk and twiddled with the mouse. Instantly the screen had two photographic images on it. One was a close-up of a young man's face. The other was his profile.

'I'm going to show you six young men. You shouldn't say anything as you look at them. After you've had one look I'll show you them again. Then if you see the man you saw getting out of the silver BMW last Sunday you should tell me. Is that clear, Miss Bell?'

'Lizzie, please,' she smiled.

The first of these was Dennis Scott. The next four were just similar-looking young offenders that they had on record. The sixth was Bradley Simon.

'You take your time, er . . . Lizzie. And if you don't recognize any of them don't feel obliged to say you do.'

'The young men who were in the car that killed the little girl are here? Among these?'

'They could be.'

Elizabeth Bell looked at each one for a long time. Then

Tony started them again. He sat quietly and waited. He smiled to himself at Dom Kennedy's comment about him having a soft spot for Bradley Simon. That wasn't true. He'd be the first one to lock him up if he thought he was guilty. But Bradley made his statement in the same way that he'd made all his statements. Breathlessly, childishly and in the end, Tony thought, honestly.

Dennis Scott was a completely different lad. His story though was wooden. He said things that just didn't ring true. Like that Bradley threatened to harm him if he came forward. Bradley didn't do things like that. Whenever he'd been involved in fights he'd always hit first and thought about it later. Tony couldn't imagine Bradley issuing a cold threat to someone. And anyway, if that were the case, why was Dennis Scott up at court on Friday, looking like he was Bradley's lifelong friend?

None of it made any sense.

'OK.' Elizabeth Bell spoke.

Tony looked up, momentarily pulling himself together.

'He's there. I know it's him. He got out of the car on my side, you see, so I had a good look at his profile. It's definitely him.' She was pointing at the screen.

'Definitely,' she said.

Tony Haskins smiled. It was Bradley Simon who got out of the car from the passenger's seat. He couldn't have been driving. It was Dennis Scott who driven into the bus stop and killed the girl.

It was good to have something go right for once.

# 30

We waited till it was dark. We drove the car along the high street and turned off towards the park. It was almost ten. When we got out I opened the back door and picked the flowers off the seat.

'Maybe we should have waited until Brad was home to do this,' my dad said.

I shook my head. I could never see Brad taking flowers to the bus stop where he had seen the little girl killed. He wouldn't do it. He *couldn't* do it.

I took my dad's arm and we walked in a curious way down the road, me holding a bunch of flowers. We must have looked like a strange couple trying to imitate some sort of wedding march. When we got nearer we slowed down.

'I just hope there's no one else there.'

'It doesn't matter,' I said. 'Lots of people place flowers at these tiny altars.'

'Not the family of the person who caused the accident.'

'Brad didn't cause the accident. We know that now.'

Tony Haskins had rung and told my dad the news. Brad had been telling the truth. After a week of lies he had finally opened up and explained how it all came about. Not that they'd believed him. How could they have trusted his word over Dennis Scott's? There had been a witness. Dennis had been the driver and had lied to save his own skin. I faltered for a moment and got a better grip of the flowers. Sweet Dennis who was rotten inside. Dennis who would lie and lie and even, in the end, offer his best friend up in place of himself.

We got to the place. The flowers had increased since I last passed by, many of them looked brand new. And then I remembered. At seven o'clock that evening it had been exactly a week since the little girl was killed. Maybe her family had come and laid fresh flowers. It was the first anniversary for them. No doubt there would be many more before the place turned back to being a bus stop. Months, years maybe before the girl's family could look or pass without raw memories making them falter.

Brad would go to prison. Not for the girl's death, but for trying to cover it up, that and the motorway accident. It was called *Perverting the Course of Justice*. Denny was facing prison as well, longer for him.

I felt a tingle of regret. I was sorry that Denny hadn't been a different sort of person. I was sorry that my brother hadn't been strong enough to do the right thing.

'Let's not stay too long,' my dad said, in a whisper, as if we were in a church. 'It doesn't feel right us being here.'

I put the flowers down and closed my eyes. I tried to picture the little girl but instead I just remembered the big lorry crashing into the other cars on the motorway.

After a few moments we turned and walked away, back to our car.

# A note from the author

Crime stories shouldn't just be about 'whodunnit'. I think that they should sometimes explore why a crime is committed, how it happened and what the consequences are. We are surrounded by 'crime' everyday in the media. I like to look at the personal experiences of my characters. It makes me wonder what I would do if I were in that situation. Anne Cassidy's books include the award-winning *Looking for jj*, and *Blood Money*.